PENGUIN BOOKS

NOT A WORD ABOUT NIGHTINGALES

Born in Bridgeport, Connecticut, Maureen Howard is a novelist and teacher who lives in New York City. Her short stories have appeared in *Hudson Review, Yale Review,* and *Kenyon Review.* Critically acclaimed for her literary virtuosity and emotional precision, Ms. Howard has distinguished herself as a writer through her novels, including *Bridgeport Bus* and *Before My Time,* and through her autobiography, *Facts of Life,* all published by Penguin Books.

Reader, here is no Priam
Slain at the altar,

       here are no fine tales
Of Medea, of weeping Niobe,

       here you will find
No mention of Itys in his chamber
And never a word about nightingales in the trees.

Earlier poets have left full accounts of these matters.

I sing of Love and the Graces, I sing of Wine:
What have they in common

       with Tragedy's cosmic scowl?

THE GREEK ANTHOLOGY

Translated by Dudley Fitts

Maureen Howard

Not a Word
about
Nightingales

PENGUIN BOOKS

Penguin Books Ltd, Harmondsworth,
Middlesex, England
Penguin Books, 625 Madison Avenue,
New York, New York 10022, U.S.A.
Penguin Books Australia Ltd, Ringwood,
Victoria, Australia
Penguin Books Canada Limited, 2801 John Street,
Markham, Ontario, Canada L3R 1B4
Penguin Books (N.Z.) Ltd, 182–190 Wairau Road,
Auckland 10, New Zealand

First published in Great Britain 1960
First published in the United States of America by
Atheneum Publishers 1962
Published in Penguin Books 1980

LIBRARY OF CONGRESS CATALOGING IN PUBLICATION DATA
Howard, Maureen, 1930–
Not a word about nightingales.
Reprint of the 1962 ed. published by
Atheneum, New York.
I.   Title.
[PZ4.H8524No   1980]   [PS3558.O8823]   813′.54
80-23693
ISBN 0 14 00.5596 7

Printed in the United States of America by
Offset Paperback Mfrs., Inc., Dallas, Pennsylvania
Set in Caledonia

The epigraph is from *One Hundred Poems from the
Palatine Anthology,* in English paraphrase by
Dudley Fitts, copyright 1938 by Dudley Fitts, and
reproduced by permission of the publisher, New Directions.

FOR DANIEL

Not a Word

about

Nightingales

I

WILL ALDRICH WOULD SAY THAT THE STORY BEGAN
at the Scholarship Bazaar which was held the first of
May. To be accurate, only Will's small part in it started
then, because their story, the Sedgelys', goes back in
time and back and forth across the ocean in a compli-
cated way—yet the Sedgelys are not extraordinary
people. Not extraordinary to Will Aldrich at any rate,
although he is the first to admit that he can no longer
judge, feeling like a confessor who has heard too many
aberrations of the human heart—not to speak of the
body. He is dean of a men's college and it's all in his
day's work—dealing with lust and pride and misery.
No, to Will the Sedgelys are not unusual.

May Day was sunny. Since the staging of the
Scholarship Bazaar is inevitable, Will Aldrich accepted
fine weather as a stroke of luck. Early May can be cold
—everyone still buttoned into winter coats—and the
faculty, in thin disguise, are forced to be good sports
and stand out in the mud for the entire afternoon. He
was the Fortune Teller last year and remembers that
he had just crawled out of his tent when he found
Anne Sedgely sorrowful and alone. "You are supposed
to be Queen of the May," he said.

"Yes, I suppose," she answered wearily, "but I have
no interest in it."

Knowing what Anne must have on her mind, he
tried to cheer her, saying that the afternoon was an
unqualified success and that she should always be
chairman of bazaars and bridges and social-teas—that
she lent her own charm and ingenuity. "It's only
through your efforts," Will said, "that I honestly find

9

this Scholarship Bazaar less boring than that of any previous year." He saw that Anne was smiling at him. "Look," he said, drawing her back a few steps so that they stood together in the gaudy opening of his striped tent, "look at the scene you have created."

They saw that the ancient oaks (which she had not designed) were touched with the first pale buds of the season, and under their boughs were set stalls and booths—much more greenly festooned. Garlands of imitation ivy were intertwined with the forsythia which Anne had forced during the past week, and she asked Will didn't it all look effective and natural draping the shaky wooden booths and card tables. In the middle of the campus a gigantic Maypole twirled, its pink, yellow, every-coloured ribbons twisting like serpents in the gentle breeze. From a loudspeaker system, cleverly concealed behind the columns of the administration building, Purcell's *Fairy Queen* charmed the air. The crowd, a mixture of townspeople and college people, "milled," Will Aldrich said, as he always hoped a crowd would mill—with a convincing holiday spirit: they gambled nickels and dimes to win useless trinkets; they ate sugar doughnuts and drank coffee and beer out of paper cups, but their real delight, the reason they came to the bazaar, was to see the costumed spectacle of dignified members of the faculty playing buffoons.

"Things are going well," Will said, but Anne bit at her lip and looked more withdrawn than ever. He knew then that she was staring into her own improbable dreams, but anyone else would have said that she was listening to the inventive coloratura, because Anne Sedgely appeared always to be engaged in some enlightening activity. While others mindlessly enjoyed their heavy, ill-baked doughnuts, she seemed to savour the music which she had selected for the afternoon. And Will wondered what it was now, what

10

newly plotted dénouement of her affairs had carried Anne off again so that her own bazaar, in which she had invested countless telephone conversations and endless committee meetings, should dissolve, disintegrate into the flat abstractions of motion and sound. It had to be, whatever she *was* seeing, more specific, more intense, to hold her so completely. A picture, he imagined, of herself and her husband and her daughter warming themselves around the hearth in Lane House, wallowing in their own security like the families in insurance pamphlets—or a picture of the Sedgelys—Albert and Rosemary and Anne—toasting each other with some grand American drink. Will knew, for he had listened so often to Anne's difficulties, that these vignettes (although they would horrify each one of the Sedgelys) were only slight exaggerations of her dream.

She was next to him, still brooding, and Will knew he would soon hear all, in detail. He would be honoured, as Anne's closest, dearest and so on friend, with every guarded, self-deceiving word, before this new event—if it were anything as definite as an event— was presented coolly, factually to the entire community. Will Aldrich studied her and thought: "How clever she is." Anne Sedgely tilted her stylish head as though she were listening to Corydon's amusing song *'Ah come love, leave these dull fools.'* Her smile was contrived.

"I don't know what's wrong with you," he said.

"Pardon?"

"I said this is an excellent Scholarship Bazaar, though *I'm* doing no business at all."

Anne turned to him: he wore an enveloping black gown which she recognised as his academic robe and a purple velvet turban. "You don't look clownish," she told Will. "You look too real, like a real wise man who can look into the future." She glanced up dis-

11

approvingly at the turban. "I thought you were going to wear that pointed hat—the one with the stars."

"It was too ridiculous."

"But that's the idea—the whole idea." She teased him: "You're no good like that. You look like our beloved dean, our white-haired prophet. Anyway I suppose it's my fault: I miscast you—or didn't give you enough of a role to play."

She reached up with graceful hands to straighten his turban, and it was then that Will thought her handsome—after all the years—lovelier then than when she married Sedgely.

"And you don't look at all Elizabethan. The theme *is* Elizabethan, you know: we have a Falstaff, and a Dame Quickly at the Boar's Head, and the boys are pitching foam rubber tomatoes at Walter Raleigh." Anne tried to sound lively, Will remembers, as though it were all such fun, but in the next moment she faced him and spoke of her real concern: "I'm sending Rosemary to Italy this summer."

"She's still a child," he said.

"That doesn't matter." Anne was convinced. "This is my first sensible move since the whole irrational nonsense began. I'm sending her to Italy to bring Albert back."

"Are you sure?" Will asked.

"Of course. She has her reservations for early June."

"Don't be simple." (For the first time he was angry with her.) "Are you sure that you want it that way, that you want Albert to come home?"

Anne Sedgely smiled thoughtfully and said in an annoying *grande dame* manner, "Naturally, I'm sure."

Then Will laughed at her: "Don't forget, don't forget what happens in Henry James."

"Rosemary isn't all that sensitive." Her reply was sharp, defensive because she couldn't see the absurdity of her situation; she couldn't laugh with him, and

12

he never will forget the sudden change, her plaintive, weak voice—"Tell me then, tell me while you're in character, what *will* happen?"

Like a master of the occult and supernatural, he rounded his hands over a non-existent crystal ball: "I see everything turning out as you want; yes, I see the Sedgelys re-united. It is the final scene of a romantic comedy."

"If only you knew how wonderful that sounds." Her face was brilliant with pleasure. Then she took his arm and led him into the crowd. "Forget your old tent," she said gaily. "Come buy me a cup of mead . . . Oh, look at that, Will. Isn't she absolutely perfect."

They watched Elaine Green at the handicraft booth playing Rosalind, and Anne said that she had not mis-cast the *whole* bazaar. She had chosen Elaine because she was the most beautiful young woman in town, and she had assigned her a role which could only be costumed in tights. And they watched Rosalind in boy's disguise reach for a paper bag, her tights stretched to the point of incredibility, and the students lined up to buy ceramics and needlework as though their very lives depended on it.

For Will Aldrich it was on May Day—his entrance into the story—though he will say, if he ever speaks of it, that the story is not his. It belongs only to the Sedgelys—to Albert and Anne and even to Rosemary —as if, Will thinks, they had constructed it upon some sacred esoteric principle so that this one thing if nothing else, this story, would be theirs.

When at the Scholarship Bazaar he saw Anne finally laughing, head thrown back, lovely long throat, and the tight muscles around her mouth softened, he asked, "Would you like to play golf tomorrow if the weather is still good—and start the season?"

'Ah come love, leave these dull fools,' Corydon be-gan again.

13

"Oh, damn," Anne said, "they forgot to turn the record."

Rosemary waited in the hot Italian sun for her father. It seemed strange that this could be his garden, unkempt and pathless, a profusion of unfamiliar flowers and fruits. She shut her eyes to keep out the burning light, to visualize the scene she expected. Her father would enter she imagined—even in this wild courtyard so far from their real home—as he had always entered their living room—to greet a colleague, a student, or a guest for dinner—with a slightly forced smile. Horribly embarrassing; she could not bring herself to blame him, but there *was* something stuffy and unconvincing about his handshake and the "friendly" look in his pale eyes. His manner hadn't irritated her until a few years ago when boys began to take her to movies and dances. Then it became deathly, really deathly: he always remembered the boys' full names, names just *no one* would think of using—Whitney, Gregory, Bradford—and their prep school or college; and then he insisted on talking about the school "teams". Oh, she shivered in the hot Italian sun . . . she could almost hear him:

"Well, Bradford, I see you certainly 'did Dartmouth in'," (he said it as if quoting from a dictionary of slang) "sixteen-zero."

"Yes, Sir." Rosemary knew he was the kind of father, the kind of professor, that boys always call "Sir".

"My, Whitney, I imagine you've had some excellent skiing in Vermont this year."

"Yes, Sir."

The feeling that she would choke, which always came to her during those painful social exchanges filled her throat now, mingling with the strange, dry heat about her. He will make me feel this way, Rosemary thought, even though we are in another country.

14

Her father, Albert Sedgely, always met people as though they were entries in an appointment book. He walked deliberately towards his guests and with a studied firmness grasped their hands and forced one of his direct, sincere looks out of his watery scholar's eyes. Then, if the guest was one of Rosemary's friends, he talked about scores and teams, because he knew that adolescent boys were interested in such things (and in automobiles, but *there* Sedgely drew the line); and it wasn't that he didn't know about the "teams", Rosemary thought; he knew all too well the name of every discus thrower in New England. He made a point of knowing but, she felt rightly, he didn't care. Yes, his meetings with her friends were deathly, horribly embarrassing; yet she could never blame him exactly because, well-informed, he was only trying to be friendly and interested.

Rosemary opened her eyes and swayed slightly. The heat was overpowering and the sun, directly overhead, cast no protecting shadows. She went towards the one wicker chair in the garden, picking her way through an entanglement of dead ivy. This garden interfered with the picture of her father, for though she could recall his gestures, even his words, it was difficult to imagine him here, in this setting. She saw an old Italian courtyard of no particular century and no particular style. There were two walls, washed with a fading Pompeii-red which extended from the rear of the house for about twenty feet and met a shabby line of small fruit trees and shrubs. There was a raised area of weathered terracotta tiles behind the house that originally had been a terrace, and Rosemary noticed that the same tile traced a disintegrated path through the yard. Now the grass and pacassandra grew right up to the back door, obscuring the terrace, and the ivy, brittle as shell, twisted over the path in great untidy clumps. Persimmons, eucalyptus, roses, and olives all grew together, one undisciplined hybrid; there was a general confusion where there had once been order. The strangest touch of all was a niche in one of the garden walls which held a new plaster statue of Christ: Christ with pretty brown curls, dressed in scarlet robes, and pulling aside the drapery on his chest to display a perfectly shaped heart, blood red, bleeding carefully onto his white undergarment. In front of this statue a vigil candle set in red glass was burning—which added, Rosemary thought, unnecessary light and heat to the scorching June day.

The shiny plaster Christ created a problem for her, not in religion, but in aesthetics. Rosemary believed that since she had seen her father—almost two years ago—she had changed completely. She acknowledged that she had been a child when her parents left for Europe ... a little girl in boarding school; then her friends were playmates really, or conspirators against an outdated ritual of hours marked off by the feminine tinkle of bells ... a bell to go to classes, a bell to eat by, a bell to sleep by. Yes, she had been a child then, and even her most recent life (in the larger world of a college dormitory) already seemed another era. Left by herself in the Italian sunlight, she felt serious and adult, burdened with responsibilities unknown to the child she had been. The woman Rosemary sighed, and to her thin lips there came the slightest smile of incredulity. All that had happened to her was so horribly *fait accompli*, but she could not conceive that these last two years could have transformed her father, a man of taste (oh, stodgy, limited, no doubt), into a man who could live with this garden and a cheap statue of whatever they called it—the Sacred Heart.

But this was her father's courtyard and he did live here, because Rosemary saw on a rotted and splintery table of crate wood, his typewriter, thick with rust, and a litter of his papers weighted by an empty wine

16

bottle and a few dusty rocks. On the ground there were discarded sheets that seemed long ago to have been glued to the earth by rain, and now to have come loose, their edges curled and yellowed in the noon-day heat. That typewriter Rosemary remembered; for many years it was set exactly in the middle of Albert Sedgely's polished mahogany desk, secured there by the traction of a special rubber pad. And always his papers were filed away, except of course a few sheets which were clipped neatly inside the manilla folder labelled "*Current, unrevised*".

The young believe that change is their particular virtue, that their elders are working off a dull purgatory for the sin of constancy. "I am not the girl I was two years ago," Rosemary thought, but she was certain her father would be as she remembered him, and to contradict what she saw, the decaying foreign courtyard with its holy statue, she unfolded the evidence of her memory, recalling another garden, the Victory Garden of her childhood. It was the first, easy association because she had helped her father plant a Victory Garden during the war, a family project that Sedgely had conceived as a small but sincere act of patriotism by which he could spend some hours each week with his child. It was a busy time for him, the war, but he felt that he could tend a garden and play with Rosemary simultaneously—a few hours away from teaching the illiterate young officers the fundamentals of sentence structure. He began their "project" by buying packages of seeds and having the soil of their smooth spring lawn tested in a laboratory; then, he had the neatly mown grass torn by a tractor, and powdered minerals and horrid sacks of sheep manure added to the lumpy earth. It could have been such a nice, satisfying garden, she thought—all the even rows of vegetables—but a little educational game was connected with the project: it was like so many

17

of her other tainted memories. Rosemary at the age of seven was encouraged by her father to memorize the botanical names of the common vegetables, and when she went into the garden with him they pulled the *allium cepa,* thinned the *daucus carota,* or perhaps if it had not rained, watered the *raphanus sativus.*

Rosemary saw herself now, a small girl in a vegetable garden trying to prop up a tomato plant . . . and she saw her father stop to hold the heavy fruit while she tied the plant to a long green stick . . . "There, that ought to support the . . ." he said, leaving a blank to be filled in. And she, still a child, quietly answered, "*lycopersicon,*" wanting terribly to say "tomatoes," or substitute the Latin name for lettuce; but she saw her father, straightened up now, towering above her with an expectant smile and that practised bright look in his eyes, and she answered "*lycopersicon,*" for him— but reluctantly, the word hardly spoken as in a dream.

It was too bad that he did things that way, because she did not dislike her father and might have loved him with a certain restraint, if he hadn't been so embarrassing to her. But that was not it, she told herself; more often than not she was embarrassed *for* him. In any case, she decided that the uncomfortable feeling that she had about him had existed long ago, even before those deathly exchanges with the boys who came to call for her. The strange thing was that other people seemed to think it was fine that she knew botanical names or could recite the forty-eight states and their capitals. To other people, Albert Sedgely was a scholar and a professor; they liked his chatty manner and immense, off-beat knowledge—about collegiate sports for example. All her friends thought he was a good guy, but what she personally couldn't stand was the way he *tried* to be a good guy. It spoiled everything.

Rosemary was getting a headache from the sun and

she wished that her father would come. The perspiration soaked through her dress, and the coarse wicker chair pressed scars into her back and legs. It occurred to her that she was the only living being out of doors. Coming up from the station in a taxi she had seen no one in the streets. All the shop fronts were hidden by corrugated aluminium blinds and the shutters on the medieval houses were closed against the heat. She became more and more angry with her father, angry that he hadn't come to meet her, that even now he wasn't here. It was a poor reception after two years, she thought bitterly—but considering what he had done to her mother, she couldn't have expected much. After the crazy way he insisted on living in Italy, practically deserting his wife and never writing to his only child, she should have *known* that he would not meet her at the station and that she would sit, locked out of his house, rotting—just *rotting*—in the sun.

When Rosemary arrived at his address, the Villa Carina, an old woman dressed in black answered the front door. Smiling and nodding, she seized Rosemary's suitcases, pushed them into a hallway and closed the door behind them. Then the old woman led her around the house, through a narrow arch into this courtyard and spoke a noisy incomprehensible monologue for two or three minutes. Rosemary understood nothing, and watched incredulously as the old woman went into the house through a back door, shutting it in her face. All that she understood was that having just arrived in Perugia after nine days on a boat and a long, filthy train ride from Genoa, she was expected to wait in this blazing direct sun for her father. She had waited for fully a quarter of an hour, and now she decided that she had been wrong about him—absolutely wrong: her instinctive feeling that he could not have changed now seemed youthful and sentimental. "Oh, he's changed all right," Rosemary said to herself, "he's crazy." Her eyes blinded, her head burning, terribly lost in this dry garden, she admitted that he might very well be different. The possibility (one that she had dwelt on often) that Albert Sedgely might be mad was actually comforting: after the crazy way he had acted with Anne not to mention leaving his own daughter in this nasty, sweaty yard—he must by this time be totally insane. As she looked around she knew that she had to be right. Here was evidence of his madness, this weedy old garden and that disgusting statue and the crumbly, positively unrecognizable terrace. It was all too crazy—and that funny old woman who kept shouting at her. Her father *had* to be mad. For months she had secretly hoped that this might be true. Now she told herself how wonderfully it would alter things: he would no longer be responsible for all the foolishness in their lives: her mother would still be a martyr (Rosemary liked that), but not a distressed, forgotten woman. Anyway, the whole situation was embarrassing, really deathly, but if her father turned out to be insane—well just a bit cracked—then there would be nobody to blame and nothing to be upset about.

Albert Sedgely, sporting a white moustache, appeared in the doorway. He hesitated for a moment; not smiling, not saying a word, a look of complete wonder on his face, he walked across the terrace to his daughter. It was *not* the scene she had imagined; he did not come towards her with his old studied confidence—the ivy, the clumps of grass and weeds formed a more difficult carpet than the oriental rugs in their living room. And in place of the forced smile, Rosemary was amazed to see a new intensity, a look of expectant, almost mystic joy—as though like some early saint he was stumbling towards the Holy Grail. She unstuck herself from the wicker chair and attempted a little smile, but before she could speak he drew her into his arms and was wildly thumping her back and shoulders (Rosemary felt that he was pounding the heat through her flesh directly into her lungs), crying, "*Cara, cara.*" Albert Sedgely was laughing, a nervous, uncontrollable gurgle in his throat.

He kissed her again and again; then he stood apart from his child, still painfully squeezing her hands in his. "*Carissima.*"

Rosemary noticed that he blinked his eyes, and drops—they must be *tears*, she thought—ran down his cheeks.

"*Mia Rosmaria, mia cara.*"

"Daddy, how marvellous you look. You're so tan."

Though she had finally admitted that her father might *be* different, it had never occurred to Rosemary that he would *look* different. The lean, greying man who had been Professor Sedgely, the ordinary academic who had been her father no longer existed. "You're *so* tan," she repeated. It was the only polite comment that came to mind; everything else about this man who had thumped her and kissed her was startling and absurd. His grey hair was much whiter than she remembered, or perhaps his skin, which was now tight and dark, made it seem whiter. He had grown an enormous moustache, tapered at the ends with an upward flourish. It, too, was white: lily, snowy, unadulterated white—yet he did not look older. His cheeks were firm; his white temples and moustache gave a new definition to his face. Rosemary blinked into his once pale eyes, which now seemed like gems set against his darkened skin, china-bright and violet. Then she glanced down and stared with increasing horror at the suit he was wearing. It was made of a striped material, like the stuff of morning trousers, but the stripes were bolder, sharply contrasting black, grey, and white. He was still slim, but the way the short double-breasted jacket stretched around

21

him suggested a paunch where there was in fact none. And he was wearing yellow suede shoes—really disgusting—pointed at the toes and with tiny holes punched in an elaborate pattern. He seemed to his daughter to be got up as a gangster, or garishly made up for a musical comedy; and how deathly, she thought, how absolutely deathly to speak to me in Italian. "*Hello*, Daddy, you certainly are brown."

"My God," Sedgely's voice boomed through the mid-day stillness, "I'm glad you've come. Let me look at you. I'm positively glad," and he emphasized his delight as though he had some doubt which only the sight of Rosemary dispelled. "Look at her," he shouted to himself. "Look at how tall she is, and that blonde hair. Why here she is from another world, all pretty and grown up. My God!"

Rosemary thought that he was very strange—and how he shouted. He had never been so ebullient at home, even in his most frivolous moments after two martinis. She wondered whether this shouting and the odd clothes were part of his "problem"; yet her mother didn't mention a moustache or prepare Rosemary for the striped suit. Anne had said that when she left him he was morbidly quiet and non-committal, that he was strangely determined to stay in Italy, that he was childishly taciturn and stubborn about his decision, but there was nothing, nothing at all in her reports to suggest a boisterous man tossing her about and pounding her back in this confusion of a courtyard. "It's so nice here," Rosemary said vacantly—"I mean the garden and all . . ."

"Ah, but this is a tragedy." His face grew solemn as he looked at the dusty earth. "It is very dry here; it doesn't rain at all, not a drop all summer. The olive trees and the vines are ruined. I'm sorry," he said, still looking down at the parched earth, as though he personally were to blame for the cruelty of nature, "I'm sorry that I wasn't there to meet you. I thought you were coming this afternoon." He stopped abruptly and cleared his throat; the apology hung uncomfortably in the air between them.

"Don't be silly," she said in an enthusiastic voice; but Rosemary was more thoroughly shocked by his embarrassment than she had been by his moustache or his tears. There had never been any reason for awkward apologies in her father's life. She remembered that for him an apology was a bit of social etiquette: he would say that he was sorry or ask to be forgiven when someone else was being difficult. In his carefully defined world he had always been sure that what he said and what he did were indisputably correct. That he could forget her train was to arrive at exactly 12:47, that there could be any doubt in his mind about this scheduled fact was inconceivable. Yet Rosemary reached out and clasped her father's hand, a gesture she had outgrown along with the cruder instincts of childhood. In his shame he was suddenly appealing. "Oh, please, Daddy, I've come across an ocean by myself. I'm awfully self-sufficient."

"No," he said, "I'm sorry. It was a dreadful mistake and then when you came—well, we weren't quite tidy inside, and that is very important in Italy, *la bella figura*. We have to look our best or not be seen at all." Sedgely laughed nervously and led Rosemary towards the house. Together they stepped into the darkness and he closed the door behind them against the sun. "It's quite small I'm afraid."

Though Rosemary could not as yet see anything, she said, "But it's nice, Daddy . . ." and again she heard a note of false enthusiasm in her voice. Gradually the room grew brighter for her, took on shape and proportion: it was plain and narrow. The walls were white-washed and the floor was a terrazzo of chipped green marble: the dark beams which ran across the ceiling and the simple furniture stood out in sharp silhouette. As she began to cross the floor her heels clicked, Rosemary thought, as though she were alone in a museum or a bank.

Motionless, Sedgely watched his daughter shift forward and steal quietly on tip-toe up to the carved stone head of an angel, and he hoped that the sound of terrazzo floors in a living room would become natural to her, but that the ornate fireplace which she stood in front of would not cease to amaze her.

She drew her fingers up the stone column, over the stylized icanthus leaf to where the cherub's head irrelevantly sprouted and supported with its baby curls the immense weight of the mantel. She found the angel charming. "How funny," she said. Yes, it *was* charming, and the room was pleasant too, but Rosemary resented the cool order here as much as she had resented the heat and disorder of the garden. Her mother had called this house a hovel . . . "a freezing, inconvenient pit."

"See," Albert Sedgely pointed excitedly to a metal cot, "here's your bed. I've put it under the window so that if there is a breeze from the yard—though it isn't likely in mid-summer."

Rosemary was sure that Anne, her mother, had to be right and that her father, Albert Sedgely, had to be wrong, so of course, however pleasing this room or this odd Villa Carina might seem to her, the fact was that it was ridiculous for him to be living here at all. For a man of his age and his position to abandon himself to this cottage on the outskirts of Perugia was wrong. In many long and analytic conversations, she and Anne had agreed that it was simply wrong and crazy.

Foolishly, Albert Sedgely bounced on the squealing springs of the cot, then jumped up to straighten a chair. He smiled at Rosemary and threw out his arms in a gesture of self-mockery, but she could see that he was proud of his arrangements and that perhaps—but it would be too peculiar—perhaps he wanted her approval. It was a bare, white room with a silly, over-decorated fireplace, and was probably, as Anne said, inconvenient, but Rosemary felt suddenly with a tinge of guilt that she was in a wonderful place. "It's a lovely room," she told her father with a conviction that surprised her.

"Come, see the rest of the house. Dear God," he looked at his child with glowing, violet eyes and repeated, "here she is and quite pretty."

Rosemary flushed because she knew (it was her one true mark of maturity) that she was not pretty. She was sleek, and might at most be considered good looking but never pretty. Her straight hair was clipped in a smooth blond cap that fitted close to her narrow head. Her face was a bit too long to be soft, and as she talked the animation of her mouth and chin accentuated the lower half of her face, protruded it, not unattractively, but so as to remind one of a finely bred and sensitive collie. She had grown tall, like her mother, with the hardly visible breasts and straight hips prescribed by fashion magazines. As she followed her father into the next room, his bedroom, she moved her thin white hands with a languid restlessness. Falling limp from the bony wrists, they were like the paws of a splendid dog, delicate and trained.

Her father's insistence on calling her pretty, even repeating the word, disturbed her. It wasn't like him to be inaccurate unless he was trying to be kind: she expected that embarrassing "good guy" tone in his voice. Still standing on the threshold of the bedroom, Rosemary waited for some remembered sign of premeditated love and paternity that would be sure to fail, but her father dashed about in his skimpy, striped suit, opening the closet door, the bathroom door, patting the pillows on his bed, smoothing the bedspread. It was pathetic to watch his demonstration since there was nothing much to put on display. True, he had completely modernized the bathroom, but in summer no water ran in Perugia so the bright chromium faucets which he turned on would not even dribble and the hot water heater was ludicrous. His bedroom was an ascetic, white box. The large bed was covered with a white cotton spread, and the austere wooden table and one straight chair were monk-like. Remembering the grace of Lane House—the serpentine chest and the delicate Sheraton bed posts in her mother's room—Rosemary could not praise this cell. She noticed a copper vase with fresh carnations on the table and said, "The flowers stand out so against the white walls."

Coming to Italy—in the isolation of her deck chair —Rosemary had determined that when she arrived she would be rational and calm with her father. Tucked in plaid rugs with a relaxing cup of bouillon, it had seemed easy—her mother had been sinned against, or, to state the case in what Rosemary imagined to be more sympathetic terms: Anne was the victim of her husband's insanity. Albert Sedgely, an ordinary, middle-aged academic, had decided to live in Europe—and that decision in itself was ordinary enough—but he had chosen to live, not in the gaiety of Paris, nor the sophistication of Belgravia, nor amid the wonders of Florence or Rome, but in the bleakness of a medieval town where, his wife said (and Rosemary knew she must be right) there was nothing but a fountain and a provincial museum. They had been travelling together, the Sedgelys, and Anne out of duty or even devotion had stuck it out in Perugia for the winter. They had lived in the cold and damp of this small villa, but then in the spring she had returned to America.

This was the skeletal plot which Rosemary knew so well. She and Anne had gone over the sequence of events so often. First, her father had decided to live in Italy and then perversely had chosen Perugia. Anne Sedgely, finally exasperated, had packed her bags and come home alone. The events were all too familiar to Rosemary, but they did not seem real. She had never heard her parents quarrel and could not visualize two controlled people fighting out this capsuled drama. When she had asked her mother in one of their "frank, adult" discussions, if they had fought, Anne said, "We didn't scream at each other, dear. It would have been better I suppose if we did—"

Rosemary only half understood the remark. She had been raised intelligently in a community of academics where conversation is an art not quite dead. She was used to implication and to understatement, but often she failed to complete those silent equations of the mind that would have told her who was implied or what inferred. She considered her awareness of the ironies of life to be a part of her maturity, but she merely knew that these ironies existed; she was unable to discern them. She arrived in Italy with meagre qualifications, with the vague outline of a story and Anne's bewildering words. A few minutes ago in the heat of the garden she had broken her first pledge: had been quite irrational, angry at the very memory of her father, and now curiously she began to find his house attractive, and with growing admiration she watched him perform.

Albert Sedgely was flailing about his bedroom, re-arranging the three pieces of furniture, laughing to himself and smiling at Rosemary with his gem-violet eyes. He bowed clownishly and with mock elegance recited a few verses in Italian. The words spilled forth in a lush rhythm of delicious consonants and mellow vowels. He translated for his daughter: it was a sticky line or two about a house which though small and poor was to the Italian *sempre*, always he said, a *palazzo*. Turning away he postured in front of a broken piece of mirror and twisted up the ends of his moustache.

He led her then to the third—the only other room in the Villa Carina—the kitchen. It seemed larger to Rosemary than the living room, with the same white-wash and dark beams, but the walls were cluttered with copper pots and moulds; red onions, garlic, pepperoncini, spices hung from the beams; baskets of fruit and bread were in the darkest corners away from the sun. Heavy crockery was set out on a long table covered with white linen. "Lovely, oh lovely," she murmured. Every corner and shelf of the rustic kitchen was dramatic, arranged with the subdued greens and translucent yellows, the exquisite lights of a *sei cento* still life. There was neither refrigerator nor exhaust fan to mar the composition. Like many Americans who come to live in Europe, Rosemary was determined to enjoy the hardships of primitive life. Predictably, and with great sensibility she wanted to savour the rancid butter and insist that warm beer is more refreshing. Rosemary thought: "Anne never mentioned this . . . all so divine and Italian." She fell in love with the antiquated kitchen.

It was extremely hot. The old woman who met her at the front door stood over a black stove stirring a big pot of soup. The sweat poured down her withered cheeks drop by drop and spat on the stove. She smiled at Rosemary and drew back a greasy string of hair from her eyes.

"Luisa," Sedgely spoke to her; his voice was much louder in Italian. He shrugged his shoulders; he ex-aggerated, waving his arms about, pointing at the table and then at his watch. He gently pushed the old woman at Rosemary, and Luisa took the girl's limp

28

fingers and crushed them with her hand. She wore a black cotton sack and colourless felt slippers. Her grey hair was drawn back from her plain sunken face in an untidy knot—the classic hair style of all European peasant women, ancient and sad. Now she began to talk, shouting into the girl's face.

"*Buon giorno*," Rosemary replied, and though she spoke in a normal conversational tone she felt as though she were whispering a secret message.

"She can't hear you," Sedgely yelled. "She's deaf . . . totally deaf." At this, Luisa who could not understand began to laugh in a hollow voice. She pulled at her useless ears and shook her head in hopeless negation.

"*Buon giorno*," Rosemary screamed, but Luisa had returned to her pot of soup, swishing the liquid noisily with a wooden spoon.

"She is a wonderful cook," Sedgely said.

"But where does she stay?" Rosemary asked, thinking of the one bedroom in the little house.

"Oh, Luisa goes home at night, and usually in the afternoon she goes home for the siesta, but today was special. There has been such a fuss about your coming." Sedgely sighed; indeed, there had been a great fuss about Rosemary's coming and he had muddled it, forgetting the time so that poor old Luisa had to stay and straighten up. Now after the excitement of greeting his daughter he was tired. He poured two glasses of white Umbrian wine and they sat at the table in silence.

As Rosemary sipped the cool wine, all the long and analytic conversations with her mother seemed distant. They had decided that she would feel the situation out and ask no questions when she arrived in Perugia. Without telling her mother, she had read some Jung and Freud in preparation and a volume that seemed more to the point, *Mental Diseases in the Middle Years*, by a Professor Jan Schöonemacher. She

29

tried to ask herself now what dreams had formulated the startling figure who sat across the table from her? What pre-conscious machinations of the repressed—or was it suppressed—sexual desire had unfolded the personality of Albert Sedgely? And from what archaic image of the primordial guilt ... It was too difficult really: none of the symptomatic twitches or external rashes noted by Professor Schöonemacher appeared on the relaxed, brown face of her father. True, he wore a gaudy suit, yellow suede shoes, and he twirled the points of that moustache, a marvellous moustache —she was surprised—how soon her eyes adjusted to his peculiarities.

Actually, when she had thought of her father during the year and a half in which her parents had lived apart, she had not thought in the language of her newly acquired and undigested psychology. She had only just finished these tomes, reading bits of them each night as though she were reading her Bible, before they put her to sleep. No, to speak truthfully she had envisioned her family's predicament in terms of justice, right, rottenness, and the annoyance to Anne and to herself. She had thought with simplicity, "Why in hell doesn't Daddy come home from Italy and stop embarrassing us?" Outside in the garden she had wondered why her father lived in this nasty little house. Now these questions did not enter her head; noticing that four places were set at the table, she asked, "Who's coming to lunch?"

"Carlotta and Ennio Manzini. They live in the next villa." Albert Sedgely spoke calmly now and told her about his neighbours and how he managed the everyday affairs of his house. He had been afraid of this meeting with his daughter. For some months he had known that Rosemary was coming to him for the summer but he tried to forget it, and had succeeded so that this noon he had missed the arrival of her train. He was ashamed of his own self-deception. He might have looked up the letter from Anne or phoned the station but he had purposely closed off that deep grey corner of his mind in which he knew that Rosemary would arrive at 12:47. When he saw her, a skinny boy-like figure, waiting for him in the garden, her narrow face turned scarlet by the heat, he was sorry that he had dreaded her coming.

"If I could have known," Sedgely admonished himself, "that I would feel . . . that this love, hidden inside would overcome me—then I would have been waiting, anxious to see my child. Astonishing—such spontaneous emotion, grabbing Rosemary like that, crying. It was a marvel : not to rehearse a smile for her, not to remind myself to place a dry kiss upon her forehead." Though exhausted by his emotions, he was gratified : it pleased him that he could explode his feelings naturally in a great voice and hear them shattering about him. Yesterday he quarrelled with Popperatti in the biggest café on the Corso Vanucci. He and the threadbare communist tailor had shouted through that same old argument on the Hungarian revolution—until he, Sedgely, had slapped *Il Mondo* against his knee in a final dramatic gesture and stomped out of the café. Later, in Popperatti's shop they stood together midst scraps of brown and grey cloth and drank a brandy to make it up. And today, without thinking, he lost control, kissed Rosemary warmly and even cried. Yes, he recalled the dry brush of his lips against her forehead; for years he had lived with this aching insufficiency, but now his emotions shattered against the walls of his house and in the streets of the town. He could hear them and see a reflection of them : Popperatti spitting angrily on the floor, or the affectionate smile that lingered now on his daughter's thin face.

"When are your friends coming?" she asked.

"They should be here now ... It's all my fault for confusing the time. Carlotta is probably ready by now, but Ennio is hard to find. He owns a motor-scooter and can race half-way to Milano before we know it." Sedgely told Rosemary again about Carlotta Manzini who lived next door and her young brother Ennio until his words trailed off wearily into silence. It had been a difficult morning.

As Rosemary watched Luisa padding about the kitchen, she let her thin hands rest peacefully on her lap and she did not speak. To her this silence seemed —well, mutual acceptance, and though she and her father had said nothing of importance to each other, Rosemary felt that her prepared conversations—news of Lane House and college—were remote and unnecessary. She had planned to tell her father several things, imagining that it would be difficult to say anything at first. Coming on the *rapido* from Genoa she had sifted through the last two years of her life for truly monumental events. She knew it would be best not to mention Anne, not right off, so she had decided, as the Italian countryside flashed by, that she would tell him about her first year at college: that she had made the dean's list and definitely decided to major in art history, and that she had spent divine weekends with Braddy Wilcox in New Haven before he cracked up his Thunderbird. Faculty salaries went up a little and Will Aldrich had manoeuvred some money out of the Ford Foundation for an economics conference. Then there was the news, not very important, about the Perkins' new baby. But now that she had seen Italy, for four hours from the window of the *rapido*, and then changed trains at Florence, Rosemary knew that the colour slides of the Duomo in Art II were a cheat Now that she sat silently sipping wine with her father, Braddy Wilcox in his dirty plaster cast and everything about the weekends at Yale seemed childish. The Ford Foundation could only be of interest to the dullest sort of people, and that baby—the Perkins were perfectly absurd—a couple in their forties, they had just produced their first child. Rosemary thought it was deathly, simply disgusting the way he, a grey-haired philosopher, wheeled his infant all over town and talked only of diaper-rashes and Dr. Spock. Yes, the Perkins were terribly funny. Rosemary giggled and the thought rose idly to the surface of her mind, "Carol Perkins," she said, "had a baby."

"How nice," Sedgely replied.

"It's a boy." But before she could tell him how stupid Sam and Carol Perkins were, her father bowed his head and asked, "How is Anne? Did she have rose fever?"

And before she could possibly remember the name of that damn Perkins kid, he had withdrawn his china violet eyes from her and tonelessly, solemnly, as if his wife were dead he had asked that: "How is Anne? Did she have rose fever?"

"Yes, Daddy; but it wasn't bad this spring." Uncontrollably Rosemary lowered her eyes too. She had broken the perfect stillness between them by speaking thoughtlessly, wantonly of home—to be specific, of that squawking child, Samuel Perkins, Jr., whom she had seen only once, outside the A. & P. The mistake was irretrievable, and in desperation Rosemary chattered on. Her speech assumed a smart, drawling rhythm that she had acquired from her college roommate, Di-Di Barnes. From Di-Di, Miss Porter's Di-Di, Rosemary had learned the trick of a modern Demosthenes and she enunciated now as though the roof of her mouth were painfully caked with pebbles. "She's simply worn out from the Scholarship Bazaar, but it was divine. I mean she really did a *marvellous* job. That kind of thing can be so dreary . . ."

Rosemary continued nervously, relating every detail

of the bazaar that Anne had organized for the Scholarship Fund. She raised her hands in a gesture of emphasis and then drooped them from the bony wrists. Her description, all secondhand, of the decorated booths in front of College Hall was embellished with "marvellous", "deathly," "dreary" and "divine". But to Sedgely, Rosemary's affectation was not annoying; indeed he hardly noted what she was saying—the bazaar, yes, that was the perfect name for the occasion. He remembered that in different years he had sold candy or played miniature golf in the middle of the campus. Dressed in one ridiculous costume or another borrowed from the theatre department, he had annually made a fool of himself: the last time it was a female snake suit left over from a production of *Back to Methuselah*—and he asked himself would he be able to do it now. He searched for a line from the play that he had once pointed out to his class, "I have eaten strange things: stones and apples that you are afraid to eat ..." Yes, that was how it went, "I dared everything and at last I found a way of gathering together a part of the life in my body—"

"Well, well, well," Sedgely said aloud to fill in a pause in his daughter's recitation.

Rosemary drawled on compulsively, "... deathly old Johnson working the taffy machine ... not half so desperate as you might imagine." She knew that the bazaar was as foolish as the Perkins' baby. If anyone had ever cared a lousy damn about it that interest had faded weeks ago into anecdotes at cocktail parties, but she couldn't stop, because God, suppose he were to ask again about her mother. It was too embarrassing. "The theme, you see, was Elizabethan, marvellous, with some dreary madrigals ..." She pawed at the air with her hands.

These affairs had never been marvellous for Albert Sedgely though he supposed they should have been.

Foolish though they were, he acknowledged now that these bazaars were a meaningful tradition—the bacchanal, the Mardi-gras (he poured himself another glass of wine)—the old and most revered professor as buffoon, a sight to bring conditioned laughter from the students; the one-day ritual, the planned masquerade of lords and servants in reversed roles. It was an ancient pattern of release; but he had never been able to really participate in this schemed revel of fools, which attempted, at least for a day, to remove formality from the human scene. He supposed that it should have been a regular Mid-Summer's Night. "Bless thee, Bottom," Sedgely smiled to himself. "Bless thee! Thou art translated!" Personally, he had always felt thoroughly an ass.

"Crêpe-paper, Daddy?" Rosemary's thin head was turned intently towards him. Her mouth and chin jutted forward. "Don't you think crêpe-paper decorations are terribly depressing?"

"Yes." He answered abstractly and without malice. "Your mother has always had a knack for organization."

Luisa, from the depths of her throat began a song. To Rosemary, the hollow notes of the deaf woman sounded a dissonant chant above the steam of the soup, "La vita è beeeella." In front of the house there was a screech of brakes. Sedgely rose, twisted the ends of his moustache and pulled at his striped jacket to prepare himself for his guests.

"Daddy," Rosemary said, "I love your moustache." She spoke softly, with sincerity, as though she were begging her father to forgive her drawling chatter, but Sedgely had already turned his back, and hurrying away from her he boomed forth a stream of joyous Italian while Luisa sang on.

II

LANE HOUSE IS EARLY NEW ENGLAND GEORGIAN. IT WAS built for Mathias Lane upon his marriage to Sarah Chapin in 1753. Mathias was a successful paper merchant but he was not wealthy, and his home, therefore, was built not from an architect's plans but from the design books of New England craftsmen. The front door, with its inset columns and swan's neck pediment is one of the most graceful early doors in Massachusetts, and it stands in delicate relief against the severe brick structure—which might otherwise seem too rational. It was never a grand house, as some of the college administration buildings were in their day, but it is pure and remains as yet undefiled: it has no pillars, fluted windows, or later Palladian details. Around the corner on College Road, the Goddard House has been chopped into faculty apartments, and the Clark Homestead—now the Sigma Phi Lodge—was violated by the fashion of turrets in the last century. Lane House is in fact unique: students and visitors are immediately charmed by the Congregational Church on Main Street, but they do not know, as all who have lived in the town know, that its New England-white style is fraudulent, a reconstruction in the colonial manner of 1926 covering a brownstone mistake. But Lane House, the one untouched landmark, has nothing to call attention to it: even the local Historical Society (they suggested a small black "1753") has not altered the neatness of its perfect American facade.

More remarkable than the preservation of their

house is the fact that the direct descendants of Mathias and Sarah Lane still live within. But there is no history of degeneracy and violence in the family: there have been no albino Lanes, no patricidal Lanes, and no Lanes with disproportionately large, baby heads. True, there was an Emerson Lane who did not grow to the height of a normal man, but he stood at the top of his class (Harvard, 1822); he later married one of the Reverend Chapin Clark's larger daughters so that things evened out remarkably well in the next generation. And in 1874 there seems to have been an "inaccuracy" in the accounts of the State Fishery Commission, which resulted in a European tour of three years for Senator Morton Lane; but on the whole the family prospered, grew tall, and stayed near to home. At first the Lanes were paper merchants, like old Mathias, but later they took mostly to the ministry or education.

All in all, it is a sound heritage, though Anne Lane Sedgely pretends to laugh at it. She exposes the Senator, her great grand uncle, as an artless embezzler, and she has unearthed the miniature of poor Emerson, his childish body grotesquely blown up by the artist to fill the tiny gold frame. "Look, we're not at all respectable," Anne says. She votes a straight Democratic ticket, and she likes—quite sincerely—the bright young Jews who come from New York to teach at the college. She does not want to be foolish about the traditions of her family or her home, and every year Anne says that she is going to buy a new car and let the place rot, for the house is too expensive to keep up and they are plagued with draughts. Still, it *is* a perfect example of early New England Georgian.

Like the red brick, the oak beams, and the slate roof of Lane House, Anne Sedgely is native material. The lines of her body are clean and straight as she kneels to weed the path of pinks in her front yard. She is a handsome woman of forty-five, and an energetic manner and a carefully applied hair tint make her seem much younger. With thin, bony hands she pulls furiously at every blade and root that does not properly belong among the pinks. Yesterday Anne finished the right hand side of the path, weeding from the front door down to the gate. Today, unconsciously demanding some variation in life, she started at the gate and is working back up to the door.

Anne wonders what time it is, but on her sunburnt wrist there is only a circle of white skin in the shape of a watch. Yesterday her watch was covered with minute particles of dirt after her gardening, so today she remembered to leave it on the kitchen shelf. She is waiting for the mail to come and thinks it is nearly time because yesterday the postman came just when she was half way down the path. Still kneeling, she turns her head and calls to Mrs. McCabe who is cleaning in the house, "Mrs. McCabe, what is the time?" There is no answer. Mrs. McCabe must be upstairs doing the bedrooms. Anne rises and shakes the pebbles from her quilted knee-pad. She walks up to the house, faces it squarely and raises her head to the open windows above. "Mrs. McCabe"—her voice is controlled and melodious as she shouts—"Do you have the time up there?" Anne hears the vacuum cleaner switched on and knows there will be no answer. She turns, and with vacant disappointed eyes looks at the tidy rows of pink flowers that form two straight lines to the gate.

Elaine Green comes down the street. She is the wife of Philip Green in the history department and has become famous in this small town for her beauty— and her stupidity. Her golden hair is tied up in a ponytail which swings in gentle counterpoint to her jaunty steps. Elaine says, "Hi, ithn't it jutht splendid?" indicating the June morning with a sweep of her lovely arms and an expansion of her young breasts.

Anne wonders why people who lisp inevitably involve themselves with so many *s*'s, and why Elaine can manage "splendid" and not the more ordinary words. Although Elaine looks like a golden child, dressed perhaps as the daffodil or the daisy for a school play, and has an almost visionary beauty this morning, Anne Sedgely can not understand why Phil Green married her. She is such an idiotic girl. "Yes, isn't it fine today!" Anne replies.

Elaine, hurrying on to a meaningless appointment, thinks, "How lonely she must be in that big house by herself—such an old block of a place—those little windows and inside stho gloomy with all that panelling of dark wood. If I had it I'd paint that woodwork white ... maybe build a picture window." But Elaine hopes that she will look as good as Anne Sedgely does in twenty years. "She must have that hair done every week—and those Bermuda shorts are linen, the ones the Woodthide Shoppe had for theventeen ninety-five."

Anne is anxious about the time this morning, expectant. A nervous feeling has settled heavily in her chest, but her stomach is light, unsure. If she went into the house she would automatically ignore the grandfather clock, a signed Clagett, which stands in the entrance hall. Its filigree iron hands have pointed decoratively to four-thirty during the whole of Anne's life. She would have to go to the kitchen to look at her watch, knowing that the mere fact of ten-twenty-five or ten-forty would not make the postman come sooner, would not assure her that among the bills, the publisher's ads, and the announcement of summer clearance sales there would be a letter from her daughter. Anne might as well return to her work. She twists her dissatisfaction into a moral attitude and it becomes the right thing to do—to return to her gardening this morning. Pulling and prodding at the earth, she seems completely absorbed in the flowers. Yesterday she was nervous all morning, waiting and waiting for Rosemary's letter which did not come; then, in the afternoon she played golf with Will Aldrich and was so distracted that she used her number four in the sandhole, ripped into the green twice, and finally shot well over a hundred and ten. The very suspicion that she is behaving like a neurotic middle-aged woman makes Anne smile, and she picks a sprig of the pinks to stick through the top buttonhole of her shirt. After all, this *is* a lovely summer day. Surely she will get a letter from Rosemary that will set things right, that will straighten out her life once more. The clear June sun filters through the old maple, dancing intricate patterns of light and shade, spreading myriad designs on the lawn—and Lane House in contrast is reserved, massive, symmetrical. It is a comfort to Anne to look at her house. Its simplicity of structure, the graceful carving above the door, form an ideal composition and she is pleased that again this spring she found the money to have the window sashes painted. Now the heaviness within her chest lightens and the lightness in her stomach flutters away. If not completely happy, she has at least consciously relaxed herself.

Of the original estate bought by Mathias Lane, Anne Sedgely's house and small yard are all that remain. Kneeling on the front path she can hear the power mower grunting up and down the lawn of the Delta Phi House no more than twenty feet behind her home. To her right the College has turned a large stretch of land (the family orchard), into tennis courts. On her left she is protected from any further intrusion by the cinder-block addition to the library. Anne does not care—naturally she believes in progress. Why, Frank Lloyd Wright (she will defend her position cheerfully) has designed the mile-high skyscraper and there are Coca-Cola barges on the Grand Canal. Things change.

"Too-ra-loo-ra-loo-ra,   too-ra-loo-ra-lee,"   Mrs. McCabe's voice pierces through the air in a raucous "Irish lullaby", accompanied by the bass hum of the vacuum. Mrs. McCabe singing an impossible song, the persistent groan of the vacuum, the lawnmower grunting and sputtering—for Anne, these noises seem the perfect background music for a modern pastorale. For the scene does have a pastoral quality, Anne decides. Not just Lane House and the big red maple are beautiful this morning: the sandy tennis courts seem neat and bright; even the cinder-blocks of the library throw off a thousand silver lights, and for the briefest moment Anne allows herself delight. She lets her manicured finger tips idle in the dirt, and shifting the weight of her body back onto her heels, she remembers for the hundredth time, but calmly now, that it is June twenty-ninth. She counts the days once again: Rosemary sailed on the twelfth; eight days to Genoa, perhaps one day travelling down to Perugia, depending on connections—that would bring her to the twenty-first. Then say two or three days to see how Albert is, and four, maybe five days for an airmail letter—that would be the twenty-ninth at the most. It is an exceptionally pleasant day, and far down the street, beyond the tennis courts, Anne sees the postman coming.

She tends to the business of weeding and tears up a plant of particularly nasty, deep-rooted crab grass. The path will look quite nice if she keeps at the flowers. "Ah, what is so rare," Anne Sedgely repeats to herself, "as a day in June? Then if ever come perfect days; Then heaven tries earth if it be in tune," but of course it would have to be a truly good poet to convince her of this and the good poets are never interested in such a simple universe.

41

It has complexities. Twenty-three months ago Professor Sedgely went to Europe with his wife. His course on the Augustan poets was bracketed in the college catalogue; an asterisk above his name led to the note, "On sabbatical leave." A few summers before, the Sedgelys had "done" the châteaux, so they planned to do cathedrals this time, travelling from Le Havre to Rouen, then to Amiens and down to Rheims. To begin with, Anne noticed that Albert seemed a bit cantankerous, but nothing that might not be caused by a change in food or water.

They stood in front of the cathedral in Rouen, and Albert read from the guidebook, " '*La cathédrale n'est pas oeuvre du hasard; elle n'est pas sortie non plus de la pensée d'un génie unique ... Elle est, dans l'art, ce que la croisade est en politique, ce que la Somme de saint Thomas d'Aquin ...'* " He laughed and said, "What a sense of excitement the French demand. It might all be quite true, of course, but only a Frenchman can write a fifty-franc guide to the Notre Dame de Rouen and make it sound like an index to the middle ages, to spirituality, to all of life."

"But it can't be true," Anne pointed to the luxuriant façade where literally hundreds of saints in flowing sixteenth-century robes were poised curvaceously beneath their lacy spires that seemed crocheted of stone. "What specifically has Aquinas to do with such a flamboyant church?"

"Oh, a good deal. You're looking at that mad décor, but the *Summa* and the cathedral ... they have an order, a symbolic structure."

"Funny," Sedgely said to himself. "Why should I argue the point with Anne? I was the one who laughed at the French critical esprit." But for some reason that he did not understand, he would not dismiss it. "The church is a cross," he said aloud. "In

42

a particular sense, the nave is the foot of the cross, the choir the head, and the transept the arms." He thrust his arms out in a foolish demonstration. "Crucifying myself," Sedgely thought, "because these simple analogies of architecture to philosophy never work—not unless you devote a life-time to them, and in the end you've either disproved the idea or killed the spirit of it with qualifications and analysis."

To Anne he said: "The cross is a simple enough parallel, but . . . in a general sense, and generalities appeal to the French, the cathedral is the collective aspiration of an age or the allegory of a period—not unlike Saint Thomas."

"Dear, dear," Anne sighed and took the book from him. She flipped the pages, *"L'intérieur, long de cent trente-cinq metres, haut de vingt-huit,'*—at least the book is not a complete loss."

"But isn't that dull?" Albert objected. "Surely one can work out a physical problem involving the weight of the stones, the stress on the ribs and the arches until it equals the length and height of the aisles, but that in itself is not the miracle of medieval architecture or medieval engineering;" he felt, contentedly, that he was giving way to fancy. "There is something more wonderful . . . the miracle is the medieval peasant-soul being drawn through the structure of the aisle to pure actuality, pure intelligence."

Fortunately Anne was deep in the guidebook report of reconstructions and additions. "Mmm, yes," she said.

"I'm sorry to admit that it is all rubbish," Albert went on. "In reality the particular soul as Aquinas would synthesize it with the particular peasant-body was, no doubt, too exhausted from hewing and hauling the stone to attain the universal if the poor fellow knew it existed."

"What's that, dear?" Anne glanced up for a moment.

"Nothing, nothing, I don't want to justify God or

Scholasticism to myself any more than I want to defend a cheap guidebook. You are quite right," Sedgely said to his wife. "Stick to the facts."

They mounted the steps of the cathedral and stood on the porch examining the ornate draping on the saints. Sedgely felt that he was cheated and could not let go of the notion that under the facile, standard manner of the French critic there lay an extraordinary truth. "What a shame," he told himself, "that the excitement of generalities is closed to us."

He brooded and in a few minutes turned to Anne, "What do you say we go to Mont-Saint-Michel?"

She was surprised. "But it's in the wrong direction. You should have thought of that when we got off the boat. We have our reservations in Paris now." Albert made no reply, and Anne, still bewildered, said, "We have been to Mont-Saint-Michel. Besides, I think of it as a fortress, not a cathedral."

"Well, we might stop at Saint-Lô." His pale eyes lit up with enthusiasm. It was just a name to Sedgely, a town he had seen on the map, yet he was fairly sure that he had seen or read of a cathedral in Saint-Lô. What he thought of was Mont-Saint-Michel—perhaps the unreality of that rock rising out of the sea . . .

"If we go ahead with our plans," Anne reasoned sensibly. She took a large silk square from her purse and tied it over her head. She respected the religions of other people. "If we go ahead with our plans and go to Paris we can travel out to Mantes and Orleans, Tours, even as far as Angers, and then the windows at Chartres certainly deserve a second look. When we get to Paris I must find something really special to send to Rosemary . . . but then," she looked at Albert and mistook his nod of acceptance for disappointment, ". . . if you're set on Mont-Saint-Michel. It just seems illogical, that's all."

"Illogical," there was the ultimate appeal. They en-

44

tered the cathedral and Sedgely turned to his wife, smiling, "Of course, Anne, we'll go to Paris."

"Besides, I went through the whole thing on the boat," she tapped her *Guide Bleu*, "Saint-Lô was bombed out."

When they were not travelling out of the city to do a cathedral, the Sedgelys relaxed in Paris. They sat in the big tourist cafés on the Champs Elysée, sunning themselves and staring at the crowds. Towards the end of September, exactly as Anne had predicted, she was tired of suitcases and public transportation and wanted to settle in a quiet place where Albert might resume his study of "Metrical Wit in the Dunciad." Partly because Paris was so expensive, and partly because Italy had been in their plans when they talked of this sabbatical year, they decided to go to Florence. Together they found the *Pensione Bella Vista* which (it amused them) faced a noisy street with a pork shop and a tobacco store. But the advantage of the *Bella Vista*, as far as the Sedgelys were concerned, was that they could rent two large adjoining rooms and have a bath of their own. Their entire "appartamentino" (as Anne learned to call it), even the bathroom, opened on an interior garden where many—it was impossible to count them—large cats squatted among the potted fronds and miniature fruit trees.

Anne Sedgely remembered that autumn in Florence with nostalgia. They bought a little Fiat, which had been carefully budgeted, so that she might go to the galleries and the shops and leave Albert to his work. She recalled the confusions of the last two weeks in October. There seemed to be an endless amount of unpacking and there was a good deal of difficulty in arranging, in pidgin Italian, for a cup of tea in the afternoon—yes, and how nervous she had been learning to drive in the undisciplined Italian traffic.

Although October *was* a bit hectic, November was

perfection. While Albert sat in front of his type-writer, she quietly read Ruskin and Berenson or drove out up the narrow curving road to her Italian lesson in Fiesole: she had arranged for an hour each day with a penniless Marchesa. With nothing to do, these studies, Anne believed, gave a pattern to her day. She would come back to the *Bella Vista* at five o'clock to find Albert looking over his notes or pecking at the typewriter. They would have tea and she would force herself to read the news in an Italian paper, working for another hour over the excited prose of a banal murder trial.

Over and over again as she set one plate, one knife, one fork—as she ate a lone meal in her empty New England house—that November seemed almost rom-antic to Anne Sedgely: Firenze, the *Bella, Bellissima Vista*. It was the last rational month of her life.

Where was the problem then—or when did it begin? At the pensione there was a lively young poet, a Fulbright scholar, who was supposedly translating D'Annunzio but seemed to spend most of his time vibrating in front of great paintings at the Uffizi or responding to what he called the humanity of the tightly-skirted Italian girls. He talked incomprehens-ibly to Albert about this humanity, about sensitivity and intensity.

Anne had said: "Isn't he young? What can he be talking about?"

Most unexpectedly, Albert had replied without a touch of irony, "Very young, a very sensitive young man."

On another occasion which Anne remembered, this boy-poet returned from a weekend in Rome, and when he sat down to lunch with them—a bit wild-eyed she had thought—he told them that he had been to visit the Keats House in the Piazza di Spagna. "It's an overwhelming place . . . to know that Shelley's

46

bone is in that small, black urn, plucked from the fire, charred, and that Keats died in that stifling, red-brocaded room ... I thought," the boy said, "that I had seen too much to *respond*, but somehow having been in that place I understand the *quality* of their deaths."

"Yes," Albert nodded. "It is a very moving experience."

When they were alone Anne said that she had forgotten all about the Keats-Shelley Memorial. "We did go there, though, years ago."

"Yes, we did. Very tourist—the death mask, last letters," he could not help laughing, "a lock of Lord Byron's hair."

"But our poet friend," Anne said, "as pleasant as he is, he doesn't *know* anything about the Romantics, do you think?"

Albert agreed, "Probably not a thing."

"Or," she continued, "about D'Annunzio either. He speaks very little Italian."

And then her husband answered—this was the odd thing to Anne—"Oh, he doesn't know the language at all, hardly a word, but that doesn't really matter."

So when she tried to think when, at what point exactly, all her difficulties might have begun, as she washed and dried her solitary plate each night in Lane House, Anne remembered the young poet and the curious scene with Albert in Rouen and thought that even in November, he had not been himself.

At other times Anne decided that perhaps, though she had enjoyed herself so very much in Florence, it had not been amusing for Albert. Sitting behind his typewriter day after day with God only knew what undisciplined thoughts racing through his mind—they were not thoughts on the versification of Alexander Pope, Anne understood that much now, not a single new idea on the uproarious caesura—so perhaps it had been dull for him in Florence. They had met a pleasant couple, the Blairs. Charles Blair was an art professor from Princeton and Edwina was his frowzy, but knowledgeable wife—not unusual people, but relaxing to be with and much like (could they have been too much like?) so many of their friends at home. They had been to dinner several times in the Blair's efficiency apartment, which overlooked the Arno, and the Sedgelys had taken the Blairs out to discover one or another little restaurant in town. Through Anne's Italian teacher, the Marchesa, they had been introduced to a number of reserved and elegant Florentines and she had been pleased to watch Albert shake hands and say "*Buona sera*" with confidence and dignity, not in the faltering, apologetic stammer of an American who is afraid to speak a foreign language. At the time he seemed to like these new people, but there was always the possibility that, for him, it had not been fun.

Often, as she scraped the bits of her unfinished meal into plastic refrigerator jars, Anne Sedgely sorted through the events of that November to determine when, or why, Albert's problem originated. As she boiled the water for her after-dinner coffee—as always, when alone, she used an instant powder from which the caffein was removed—the occasions of Albert's strangeness suggested themselves to her, or she consciously re-interpreted her former observations : he was not odd, he was bored; he was not bored he was disturbed and perhaps questioning . . . but what?—the values of his life—a pretentious phrase; she struck it from her mind.

Whatever ideas had possessed him, it was clear to Anne later that Albert had not been worrying out the iambs of the heroic couplet in its highest development, though he sat in front of his typewriter most of the day and she had glanced at his notes as she tidied up the room ... "Alliteration, re: heavy, monosyllabic words in the carefully balanced line, as in: ..." a long listing of book and line numbers followed ... or the card which had been crossed out and thrown in the direction of the waste-paper basket, "The O.E.D. gives the reading 'magazine', which would make this (I, 32) a regular masculine rhyme." There were a few typed sheets which Anne presumed were the beginning of his MS: the facts in his speckled cardboard filing case were being selected, interpreted and set down. How could he have faced the typewriter each day, with books and notes placed directly in front of him, and never have mentioned that his work was not going well—that he had, moreover, not the slightest intention of writing his article. His articles had *always* been written in the past: the facts seemed to arrange or compile themselves almost genially for Albert; hardly a chore. And how could she have known, because when she had asked during that November how his article was coming along he had nodded and said, "Fine," just as always, just as he had always said it, "Fine"—for twenty years. How could she have known then that he was sitting, cat-like, blinking into space, his mind suspended somewhere—Anne could not guess where. He had squatted inscrutably and stared into the garden for a month—and seen nothing as far as she could tell—not even the fern leaves surfaced with their ripening reproductive cells. How was she ever to know? They had lived as always; speaking, dressing, eating in a way that was, at least to her, quite customary.

But at the time—this was an unkind memory to Anne—she had glanced at the note re: the alliterative effect in the monosyllabic word and thrown out the information supplied by the O.E.D. re: the pronunciation of magazine in 1729 and thought, "Albert is working too hard. Why he might as well be home or, God forbid, in the British Museum."

She remembered saying to him, "Don't overdo. You must have *some* vacation." And so *she* had suggested —this was the bitter thing to Anne—that he work as usual during the week—naturally, she too had her schedule—but on week-ends they should go off on a short tour—a real jaunt. Albert seemed to like the idea, because he bought the map, one that was larger and more detailed than the map in their Blue Guide.

"Yes, you have been working much too hard. We must get out more." Anne traced a thick blue highway printed over the Umbrian hills with her delicate finger. "Imagine," she said, "we have never been to Siena ... wouldn't it be nice to take the Blairs; they'd know simply everything."

Her finger sought out another highway, in red, which ran from Florence down to Arezzo, Assisi ... lots to see there; and then ... Anne recalled distinctly that she had noticed Perugia last. This was the irony compounded, that *she* had decided Perugia might be worthwhile: Perugino, the master of Raphael, Perugina, the rich Italian chocolate—her long finger trailed back an inch on the red highway from Assisi and settled on Perugia.

And so the weekend tours began to get Albert away from his work, though his mind during the week was still suspended in space—a space without the foliage of the *Bella Vista* garden that he stared at, without the cats which he did not count, certainly without the *Dunciad*—but a space of his own imagining, peopled and planted with the thoughts that Anne would never know. And how could she have known anything then, without a clue, things seeming to be as she had always known them.

That perfect November ended. On the first weekend in December the Sedgelys drove to Siena with

50

the Blairs—all four of them crowded into the little Fiat. From Charles they learned a good deal about the almond-eyed madonnas. Edwina tramped them across the *Piazza del Campo*, across the beautiful shell-shaped piazza, in her ground-gripper shoes, and marched them into the *Palazzo Publico* where they thrilled to the masterpieces of Simone Martini. On the second trip they went to Arezzo, mostly to see the Piero della Francesca's, though Charles Blair insisted that Signorelli should not be ignored.

But on the third weekend Edwina Blair had influenza, so the Sedgelys went to Perugia by themselves arriving just a few days before Christmas. The small city set high in the Umbrian mountains was cold and damp. The ancient houses were massed together, heavy and complex, like a gargantuan grey boulder, a geological structure that opened to form not streets really, but passageways through the stone. However picturesque, these medieval alleys were narrow and steep and they caught the winter wind in fierce currents. After twenty minutes of climbing up and stumbling down hills, Anne was gasping, "Oh, let's find our way . . . back to the main square. It's the only spot . . . that is on one level."

Albert started to say something, but unexpectedly a motor scooter shot out of an alley and veered towards them—an entire family mounted on the little Vespa, the young father hunched over the handlebars, his pregnant wife riding side-saddle behind, and a baby squeezed between them, hovering in air where there was no seat at all. The family balanced on their scooter like one body, as though it were a completely natural act, avoiding disaster and the Sedgelys by an inch. Anne and Albert laughed, a little hysterically, with relief. He began to speak again but the wind shrieked down the narrow cobblestone street so that Anne could not hear him.

He shouted to her: "I thought I'd like to take a walk." Because his simple statement sounded ponderous and important called out above the wind, Anne began to laugh again. The wind stung her cheeks and her eyes filled with tears. She was to remember this scene clearly—how she had laughed and cried at once as though she were involved in a melodrama.

"I'm so cold, dear," she shouted back at him good naturedly. "I think I'll find the main square and go to the picture gallery."

"All right," he said. "I'll see you back at the hotel." The excitement of their near accident and their nervous laughter had carried over into this parting: it was gay. Albert Sedgely, his ears scarlet, his coat and trousers flapping against his legs, had smiled cheerfully at his wife and waved good-bye.

As soon as he had turned from Anne he was afraid, trembling, "If I could fool myself," Albert thought, "imagine I was coming down with something— Edwina's dismal flu or *mal de touriste*, but there is nothing wrong with me—only a few impossible ideas that's all, romantic notions that make me walk in the wind like an idiot." But he felt his legs trembling and the pulse in his neck beat furious, stirring, as he walked through the unknown streets, turning a dark corner, going down a few steps—walking without direction in order that he might think. He admitted that thinking might be dangerous in such a state, but he was helpless before the attraction of his own ideas. He assured himself that this was all he had been plotting during the long, soul-searching hours at the *Bella Vista*—nothing more than a bracing, solitary walk and wasn't that foolish, heroic enough for a meek, ageing professor—marching into the wind he would probably catch his death. He puffed his way up a perfectly ordinary medieval street with underwear and sweater shops and an expresso bar, and stepped through a small arch to find himself suddenly outside the city walls.

Sedgely stood for a moment and complimented himself. So far on his little stroll—no more than five minutes at the most—he had concentrated intensely on the bearing walls of the damp stone houses, amateurishly guessing at their age, or he had further avoided the fantasies which had taken over his life of late, by observing very closely the cheap knitwear in the shop windows or squinting his watery blue eyes to discern the real difference, if there was any, between the bag of coffee beans labelled *Tipo-familia* at 240 lire per etto and the beans labelled *di lusso* at 290. Sometimes when he played this game of complete concentration he could occupy his mind for as long as fifteen minutes and never once be subject to the wild and romantic notions which increasingly obsessed him (oh, he was quite conscious that he was getting worse) for the past two months.

Albert Sedgely could see that a broad asphalt road led away from him and away from the ancient wall down to the modern apartment houses, to the railroad station, and the cinema of the new city below. There was no point in going down there, but he noticed with relief that if he went along a footpath which followed the contours of the city wall he would come to another arch, a large portal, about two hundred feet away. He planned to walk through this gateway and into the city again, deliberately concentrating all the while on the shop displays, the children, the dogs, the automobiles, so that the strange illogical force that threatened to control him might be beaten down—so that he might find his way back to the sure world of the hotel and Anne. He could hear himself asking the desk clerk, very efficiently, if the American lady had come in. If she had not, he would go out directly to the picture gallery—and Anne would talk at him enthusiastically about the paintings; he could be certain of that. Yes, it would be all right. He walked briskly along the footpath towards the high portal in the wall, quite assured that he had nothing to worry about, that by his deliberate concentration he would control the fancies of his mind until he returned to Anne.

But the gate when he reached it was the Porta Marzia, a striking Etruscan portal of the Third Century that had been incorporated into the medieval wall. It did not lead back to the city of Perugia, to the hotel at all. A slick little man with his black hair combed into deep marcels and wearing an artistically mended plaid suit stepped out of the shadows and presented Albert Sedgely with a pink card that read, "Il tour de Porta Marzia and the Via Baglioni—by your guide, Signor Luigi Rocetti."

Panic came over Sedgely, not because Signor Rocetti had appeared so unexpectedly, bowing and offering his pink card, but because his safe and orderly plans had fallen through. He looked into a dark, cavernous place that was unknown to him and wonderously inviting.

"*No, no, grazie.*" He attempted to give the card back, but the Italian guide smiled eagerly—cajoled, gently pulled him closer to the opening in the wall.

"*Molto, molto interessante.*" Signor Rocetti spoke with a patronizing tone to Albert, as though he were dealing with a frightened child, and indeed Sedgely was frightened, for suddenly he imagined the guide as a spectre who might lead him into another, terrifying world. He had not purposely sought out the Porta Marzia as an attraction of the medieval town: his being there was a casual mistake, but it seemed that he was literally drawn into this strange situation, that Signor Rocetti had pressed waves into his black hair and dressed in his carefully patched suit each day to wait especially for him, Albert Sedgely, until he should arrive in late December—a most unlikely time of year for tourists.

"No, no," he repeated, but the Italian's hand was firm on his wrist and they stepped through the portal together. There was a metallic clanking, then a scratching and in a moment Rocetti stood with a burning kerosene lamp held high above his greasy head.

"You-come-please-thank-you." Rocetti decided that it was best to try his few English words on the fellow. He seemed to be an American, in which case it was always smart to use his English words—though this fellow was not an easy case. He might be British —the suit was dark and well-cut, the back held stiff and sure—and with an Englishman he never spoke his "You-come-thank-you-please". They always wanted to hear Italian spoken fast as though they understood. But the shoes, ah, yes—too clumsy and the doggy way the fellow followed him now: he was American all right.

Signor Rocetti stood in an enormous stone-vaulted room and began his lecture. Having exhausted his English, he spoke in what he presumed was a simplified Italian, using infinitives, leaving out prepositions and pronouns, repeating the nouns and adjectives slowly. He began with the Etruscan origins of the city of Perugia, though they had nothing whatsoever to do with the Via Baglioni, an underground street built by the powerful Baglioni family—except that a few decorative statues and columns of the Etruscan Porta Marzia had been set into a 15th century wall. Rocetti, however, thought it necessary that the tour go on for at least twenty-minutes so he began by repeating *"Arco Etrusco, muro etrusco, etrusco,"* and included all the bits of historical misinformation at his command, ending usually with the rise of Fascism and his own glorious role in the Second World War.

He need not have troubled himself, for Sedgely was busy with his own thoughts. For weeks now he had known that a moment of decision must come, but he had played against it skilfully. At the pensione in Florence he had worked out a little system which began each day with a feeble study of his notes and wandered inevitably and irrationally to an examination of his past life. While Anne was out buying tooled leather or straw mats or taking her daily Italian lesson he reviewed incident after incident in his life. He had, within a week, run the gamut of his memories, listlessly circling back to recall again some mild disappointment or a tempered delight. He searched, naturally enough, for some truth and came to realize that his memories were dreary beyond reason. His was not an inspiring past—though he could claim no obvious failure as a basis for his personal tragedy—no, here he corrected himself; not tragedy, bathos—his personal bathos, trivial and anti-climactic. He saw himself realistically as a middle-aged man who had more than fulfilled his youthful promise, but then this promise, he felt, was hardly of heroic proportions. The young Albert Sedgely had been merely a bright student destined to be a capable teacher, and an eighteenth century scholar who would "continue to publish."

"*Agusta Perusia.*" Signor Luigi Rocetti set his kerosene lamp on the rocky floor so that he might use his hands freely to point out the prominence of Perugia in the Roman Empire. "*Antichità, antichità,*" he chanted and threw his shoulders up in a rhythmic movement, and then pointed dramatically to the simple stone vaulting overhead. These foreigners expected gestures from an Italian, some notion they had picked up from the peasants of Sicily and Calabria who had all gone to America—a squat race from the South with dark yellow skin—filthy little monkeys,

Rocetti thought, who spoke a monkey chatter that no decent North Italian could understand—these people of the big gestures had Spanish blood, Arab blood, *un po'negro in somma*. Well, Rocetti didn't mind the indignity of this association. He worked hard for his tips—and gestures were a part of his job—besides no one saw him: he was underground. But his perfect imitation of the Sicilian type was wasted: the American understood nothing. He tried once more, reaching back, back with his arm into the historic air to catch some bit of the Roman origins of Perugia. He grabbed it—the forgotten defeat of Lucius Antonius—with his nicotine and garlic scented fingers, that he might bring it—the blood smelling victory of Caesar Octavianus —directly under Sedgely's aloof nose. *"Una grande città, molto vecchia."*

"Ah, si." Sedgely smiled directly at his guide to cover his remorse—not a remorse for the brave armies of Antonius trapped within the walls of a burning city —but the remorse of his personal success. He was a full professor now at a fashionable New England college and had written monographs of more lasting value than were anticipated of the bright, young student, Albert Sedgely. For over a month at the *Pensione Bella Vista* he had played his little game, sitting behind the typewriter, reading over the First Book of the *Dunciad*, shuffling through his speckled cardboard filing case for a note on feminine rhymes—a whole pattern of busywork which he had set up as a defensive move against the frightening idea that he must change his life. Actually, while he had flipped through the pages of Pope he had read himself quite accurately—during November and the past three weeks. Through a mist of self-pity he had discovered himself as a greying, pleasant-looking gentleman of fifty with alert though pale eyes, professionally successful— within the bounds of reason and circumstance; a solid

teacher and an established scholar. He was, as a man, someone with a faintly comic name, Albert ... not the name of a darling Prince Consort in dashing tartan, but the name of some little man; stiff, neat, slightly mechanical in his ways whom everyone wanted to slip on Bergson's stumbling pebble ... oh, but this Albert, Sedgely admitted, never did slip. He disappointed himself and his audience by stepping cautiously to the side of that perilous pebble at every opportunity. Sedgely: the ridiculous combination of the hard plosive d with the soft plosive g: stodgey, sludgey, hedgey ...

But he saw that these latent absurdities of his name were suppressed by the correctness of his life. As an instructor at the fashionable New England college, he had met and married Anne Lane, the attractive, bright daughter of a very good family. He had loved her as well as any ordinary man loves his wife, and they had lived from the very beginning of their marriage in Lane House, her home—original Georgian, shady lawn, superb antiques, and fine silver—all that sort of thing. He and Anne had one child, an awkward, elongated girl named Rosemary, whom he tried very hard to please, though Sedgely suspected that he had failed in recent years. Rosemary's selfconscious adolescence strained even his over-developed sense of parental affection. But aside from the normal difficulty of "relating" to his child (he regretted the usefulness of the language of social-scientese), his life had progressed from one year to the next without a hitch. His academic promotions came regularly and at the proper time, just rewards for his efforts: he had not been asked to leave his post because of dullness, unpopularity, or incompetence, but then he was never beseiged by admiring students breathless for his latest *bon mot*, nor was he called to fill a chair at Yale or Harvard.

Suddenly, Sedgely became conscious that a thousand years had passed him by. Signor Luigi Rocetti was well into the eleventh century and Perugia ruled supreme over all of Umbria. Cortona, Assisi, Gubbio, all trembled at her might, all sought her protection, and Rocetti's voice had grown sharp and agitated, *"Città forte, fortissima,"* he snapped. Never, never in his life had he been so ignored, even by his sour wife, even by his pompous brother-in-law. Rocetti stood erect and brought his heels together with a commanding click, bowing, ushering the stupid American into another vaulted room of the same proportions, built of the same drab stone.

"Molto forte, molto interessante," Sedgely replied. Encouraged, Signor Rocetti mounted a stone block, and illuminated with his flickering kerosene lamp a narrow window through which the enemy might be seen, a window just wide enough to pour hot oil on the poor creatures crawling up the mountainside— just like watering the flowers, he said, and emitted through thin, blue lips a sinister laugh. This joke he considered the most original and delightful bit of his tour and even the foolish American could not resist: the American laughed ... the fellow was an idiot, true, but why should Rocetti complain. It was three days before Christmas and he had expected nothing, and now came the well-dressed American after he had picked his teeth for six weeks in the shadows of the Porta Marzia and no business at all. With renewed spirit he jumped down from the window, pressed in the waves of his hair with a practised hand, and dashed forward into the fourteenth century: the popes were off to Avignon.

The histrionics of his guide did not bother Sedgely in the least. It was all the same to him now, whether he listened to a fakir distort the centuries or to Charles and Edwina Blair run through their precisely dated lecture on the Sienese School. Listening carefully to the Blairs' disection, brush stroke by brush stroke, of a Lorenzetti triptych had also been a diversion from his thoughts, part of his conscious sport. He had played against himself and given in to himself when he had entered this fortress—or was it an underground passage—he was not at all sure about the identity of the place he was in, and clarity was not one of Luigi Rocetti's concerns. Anyway, Sedgely thought, it no longer mattered. The game was over and he had been led by Rocetti, by himself, into this dark and cave-like trap to decide. It became obvious to Sedgely then that he would not seek out Anne at the hotel or follow her to the picture gallery. He would not study with myopic eyes, the watery eyes of a man who has read too closely, the Nativity, Crucifixion, Saints in Attendance—the subject was of no importance—by Pietro Vannucci, called *il Perugino*. He would not retreat to Firenze and the *Pensione Bella Vista* to analyze the metrics of the *Dunciad*, a pedant's subject in the first place which would never be immortalized, moreover, in the excellent mock footnotes of a genius. So, although he had lost his game—the game designed as a protection against his desires—he had after all played with himself, and therefore he was the victor too—championed, cheered, carried high by the screaming, happy crowd of his own heart and soul. What a relief to speak the words, though silently of course, "heart," "soul," without the mocking censorship of mind pointing out that the heart has an organic function and the soul has neither a ventrical, nor an aorta, nor a pulpy mechanical mass to inconvenience the human body.

Who could have known then—certainly not the solitary witness, Luigi Rocetti, writhing and twisting his limbs in an epileptic effort to get a few hundred lire out of the unresponsive, dignified, nearly English gentleman—that Albert Sedgely allowed for the first moment in his adult life the awakening of a heart that *was* more than a delicate pump. But even this sense of enlightenment depended on the great decision: that he could be and would be a different man.

Now it is most important to understand that Albert Sedgely did not have a "vision" in the large stone rooms of the underground fortress in Perugia—no Christian apparition: cross in the sky, voice of God, no sudden and complete revelation of Truth, Goodness, Light ... nor a negative vision like that of the Buddhist, who, we are told, hears the meaningless echoes of all values, Good and Evil. Nothing *happened* to Albert Sedgely at all: it is important to know that. He was neither blinded by the flickering kerosene lamp nor nauseated by the rancid floral odour of Rocetti's hair grease, so there is not a touch of mysticism in his story. He made up his mind, rationally, after full consideration of the danger. The moment of insight, or whatever Albert Sedgely termed his decision, was self-inflicted; it did not involve any universal values except that he would train himself now, as a man of emotion and feeling, to experience many things—love, hate, the very extremes of a passionate world. And when he provoked it—the moment that was to change everything for Albert Sedgely—it was not fire in his breast or music in his head that came to him, but a curiously anti-climactic metaphor: he had taken life, an immeasurable, rich fabric and snipped it away, cut it down to his size. At this time Sedgely had no idea what he would be in the future, but he rejected completely the dull garment of his past.

Two noble families of the Italian Renaissance, the Baglioni and the Degli Oddi, fought on for the control of Perugia. Signor Rocetti had arrived, wearily, at the fifteenth century. He placed his lamp on the floor and stuck his hands into the pockets of his gaily checked trousers. He frowned with disappointment, "Tch-tch-tch." The American was watching him now so he repeated the mime . . . he shook his head and searched his trouser pockets—to find nothing once again. "Tch-tch-tch," bewilderment, dismay registered in the deep-set eyes of Luigi Rocetti. He smiled hopefully at the American and began to search the pockets of his checkered coat. "Ah," he sighed with great relief and produced a dog-eared pack of the cheapest Italian cigarettes. With a bow he offered one to Sedgely, but to his great astonishment and dishonour . . . *"Oh, Signore, mi scuse, mi scuse."* The pack was empty.

"*Non,*" Sedgely hesitated, "*non fumo . . . non fumo.*" Yes, that was the verb from the Latin *fumare*, he presumed, to light . . . or *fumus-a-um,* odour.

"*Peccato,*" Rocetti hissed. The trick was foolproof: he pulled out his flat package of *Nazionale* cigarettes and offered one to his client, knowing of course that it had long been empty. Naturally the ordinary tourist responded by offering Rocetti one of his own cigarettes, a good English Player, perhaps a long American cigarette, or one of the better Italian brands. Ah, well, he might have expected that this stupid, wooden fellow would not smoke . . . would not do anything, for that was how he looked, like a man who did not drink much wine, could not go to bed with a woman. How could he, Rocetti wondered, lay a hand on a woman or enjoy a litre of wine with those cold pale eyes?

"*La familia Baglioni era molto brava.*" Rocetti did not bother to pick up his lamp. He leaned against a grey stone pillar and with an air of infinite boredom recited the only part of his lecture that was pertinent to the underground fortress. The most interesting rooms were yet to be seen but the guide had decided that Sedgely was not worth his time, not in fact *simpatico*; therefore he would not lead him down the narrow "street", the via Baglioni, with its small subterranean houses and shops. He would not show him the family ballroom, the family dining room—very unique, but really not worth it to exert himself for this distant, non-smoking American. He had done his best after all with the two large, drab anterooms and he would now put a quick end to it. Not suppressing his yawns, Rocetti listed (with little regard for chronology), the warriors, artists, poets, heroes, horsemen, and great lovers of his city: *"Braccio Fortebraccio, Guido, Astorre, Braccio il Secondo, e finalmente Malatesta il Quattro. Il Rinascimento, Rinascimento,"* he chanted.

"Ah yes," Sedgely veritably glowed within, "Renaissance Man." It was somehow so fitting that this unctuous little person should mention, all unwitting, the greatest achievement of the human personality. "Yes," Sedgely said to himself, "that is it after all: the man without limitations."

Rocetti ushered his customer back to the first vaulted room and out into the daylight. He would say nothing of Malatesta's last tragic battle against the forces of the Farnese Pope—the blocking of passageways, doors, windows, to convert the Via Baglioni into a Paoline fortress. He would not tell of Perugia itself, proud city and the last to succumb to the great ambitions of the Vatican empire. The American was not deserving of all this. No, nor would he relate with customary wit and charm his unsurpassed version of Mussolini's inglorious visit to Perugia in 1938. He bowed. He smiled, and Sedgely absently pressed a thousand lira note into his greedy palm. "Not," thought Signor Luigi Rocetti ungratefully, "out of his heart but out of ignorance." The gentleman was no doubt unfamiliar with Italian currency.

The Perugians, bustling about in the windy streets a few days before Christmas, were surprised to see a brisk, bright-eyed American gentleman weaving, almost dancing, in and out and around their medieval houses. Sedgely bounced into the hotel, ordered a drink and waited for his wife. When she arrived, calm, smiling, her beautifully groomed head filled with clever and correct judgments on the paintings she had seen, Albert said in a voice, cheerful, loud, and unfamiliar to her, "Well, well, my dear. I have decided that I like it here. I think I will stay."

"Yes, of course," Anne said without thinking. They had already taken a room for the night. How could she have known what he meant? In the heartbreaking months that followed she repeated the words to herself many times, *I have decided that I like it here.*

The next morning the sun was bright, and Anne Sedgely, thinking how fine it would be to ride back to Florence on a sunlit winter day, began to pack. As she watched Albert remove his shaving cream and razor from the suitcase she remembered his peculiar words of the night before, *"I think I will stay,"* and yet they still had no specific meaning for her.

"On Christmas we are going to dinner with the Blairs," Anne reminded him.

"You go, Anne." He answered her gently.

The entire incident was so odd that Anne was not really amazed by Albert or his behaviour, but she was annoyed. Her mouth became sharp, her movements more decisive as she folded a skirt and collected her cosmetics from the dresser. "But Albert, tomorrow is Christmas Eve ... we were going to Fiesole ... we have promised the Marchesa ... Albert, if we don't start back today we will be exhausted."

"Please go if you want to," he said and took his neatly-folded pyjamas from the bag. Whether it was the strangeness of his words or the evenness of his tone, Anne did not know, but she realized suddenly and with horror that Albert meant to stay in Perugia, not only for Christmas, not for a few days, but for weeks, a month perhaps. "This is simply incomprehensible. You're ridiculous, Albert."

He unpacked a white shirt and did not answer.

"All your notes are in Florence," she pursued him around the hotel room with bewildered eyes, her voice high-pitched, imploring now : "all of your manuscript, our clothes ... Albert, this is a nasty, freezing little town ... Albert, this isn't like you."

"This isn't like me at all." He smiled mysteriously, as though he had stated a truth, sacred and beyond contention. He flourished his white shirt in the air and from the closet drew a hanger that was shaped like a cross which he held, fanatically, above his head. His pale blue eyes gleamed, "*This* may indeed be like me," he said and crucified his shirt.

"Dear God!" Anne Sedgely turned from her husband in disgust and left the room. Clearly, clearly, she recalled that glass of sweet vermouth. She had gone downstairs to the bar to think, to control herself— and in her distraction she had forgotten to say cocktail, martini *cocktail*, when the boy took her order. She hated the sweet wine, the bitter-sweet apéritifs of Italy. It was important though to be calm, to realize what had happened between them, or more accurately, what had happened to Albert.

They had been married—it would be twenty-one years next August, a long time and without difficulties. Although Anne Sedgely's thoughts were rather muddled, she was certain that she and Albert had lived through only the usual disputes and incidents : about Rosemary's education or the orange evening dress— he had said that she looked frumpish, but it was ages ago—and they had sold the property; the Lane Orchard had been levelled into tennis courts so that

65

Rosemary could be sent to boarding school, and she had given the orange dress, hardly worn, to Mrs. McCabe's daughter.

It was really confusing of Albert to assert himself in such a dramatic way when nothing at all was the matter: her own husband behaving like this, a normal, middle-aged man, an intelligent man. Perhaps a slight nervous breakdown, Anne thought ... But why here in Perugia? Why in Italy? ... It just was not credible and besides they were so relaxed in Florence at the *Bella Vista*—it had been such fun. In the neon and plastic fittings of the hotel bar she drank the sickening wine and decided, reasonably, that she must have a plan for the immediate future. She knew that she must hold her anger and her fears in check, that she must not challenge "poor Albert" (the patronizing adjective came easily to mind) or his strange behaviour. She would go upstairs to him and cheerfully unpack. She finished the bitter syrup and calculated the tip correctly, leaving a few extra ten lira pieces for the holiday season. Smiling, she gracefully walked across the lobby and rang the bell at the desk. There she sent two telegrams with exactly the same wording—one to the Marchesa in Fiésole, another to the Blairs in Florence: "Albert under weather. Afraid trapped. Buon Natale. Anne Sedgely."

When it became quite clear that Albert would not leave, Anne did the only sensible and understanding thing. She went to Florence, gathered their belongings together and re-settled in Perugia. "*I like it here.*" He had said no more than that, ever. Soon she found that she could not talk to him without bringing on another scene; coat hangers like crucifixes, inscrutable looks from him, and embarrassing lines theatrically delivered, about—well she was never quite sure what he meant at these moments. "I have a commitment to myself, Anne," he said once. Their lives took on a stagy quality and each morning she felt that she was awakening to another act of an interminably long and dull experimental play, a play that destroyed the dramatic unities and substituted no structure of its own, a tedious, arty farce that would never end.

In February she wrote to Rosemary from the Villa Carina, "Your father and I have moved into a house with a mocking name. There is a wood stove and very little else. I am not sure you would like it here ... dampness, and smoke on the walls." The picture gallery in Perugia was small and Anne soon exhausted its limited collection, but there was a course in Italian at the University for Foreigners and she was able to organize her day around the grammar drills in the morning and the conversation classes in the afternoon. Albert shuffled and re-shuffled his notes, opened and closed his Twickenham edition of *The Dunciad*. She would return from the University and find him happy, his newly-bright eyes staring into space—withdrawn. And somehow Anne had the good sense to know that Albert was just fine, that psychiatry (her first thought) would not have helped, and that after all their carefully laid plans, this was the manner in which he actually preferred to spend his sabbatical year. As far as she was concerned there was no change: he walked about the town a great deal; he bought books of Italian poetry—D'Annunzio, Carducci, Leopardi, and a scholarly edition of Dante, but never cut the pages. Spring stirred in March and the countryside promised to be lovely, but Anne could stand it no longer and she told him that she wanted to travel—to see what she had come to see. By this time it was understood without a word between them that she would go alone. Anne packed all her clothes, her Italian grammar books, her pieces of pottery, her Florentine *objets* and left for Rome.

In a few weeks she telephoned to him. "It's wonderful here, so much to do, Albert, so much to see," she said hopefully.

"Fine. Fine. I'm glad you're enjoying yourself. Rome," Albert sounded vague and detached to her, "is a beautiful city."

"Well, how do you feel?"

"I never felt better."

"You couldn't come?" she asked.

"To *Rome*?" Now Anne thought his tone was shock, disbelief as if she had asked him to rocket off the earth. They said nothing to each other for a long while and in the end Albert spoke: "You understand that I like it here. I am settled in."

The next week Anne Sedgely booked a passage from Naples and returned to America alone. What her husband needed she imagined was a few months of solitude—to be independent, to think, to write. It was certainly best, Anne assured herself, to retreat at this point, to remove herself from what might become a difficult scene and a scene in which she seemed to act no useful or constructive part . . . and yet nothing had happened, nothing much. If it hadn't been so embarrassing it would have made her laugh, the simplicity of the situation: they had never fought. They had lived together as usual in Perugia, Albert remote and introspective yet strangely excited, while she was calm. Once or twice in the night, when Lane House creaked with loneliness, Anne felt that she had been dismissed. "*I have decided that I like it here. I think I will stay.*" For eighteen months Albert Sedgely had not left the small mountain city of Perugia and in the college catalogue his courses were again bracketed and the asterisk above his name directed one to a curious note, "On leave." No date was given for his return.

"Over in Killarney many years ago . . ." Anne

whistles along with Mrs. McCabe and the vacuum. A marvellous June morning and the mailman is coming towards her. He is almost past the tennis courts and Anne thinks that if during eighteen months she has been self-contained at all times, then why not now when the letter from Rosemary is practically in her hands? She smooths her neat brown hair; a thin, tall woman, she does not look her forty-five years as she kneels weeding the path of pinks which lead from the front gate up to Lane House. There is great satisfaction for Anne in planting and growing flowers for her remarkable Georgian home. The handsome old bricks are a comfort, a palliative to her weary nerves.

The front gate opens but Anne does not rise. Deftly, she picks two pebbles from the flowerbed and turns to greet the postman with a smile that is gracious, unconcerned.

"Good morning, Mrs. Sedgely. Only one," he says and holds out the red and green striped airmail envelope of Italy.

"Good morning. You're so wonderfully punctual." Slowly she reaches her lovely hand out to receive the letter. "Why how nice," there is a touch of surprise in her voice, "It's from my daughter." Suddenly the ache returns, the unbearable tightness in her chest and with it the bottomless, shaky sensation in her stomach.

"The flowers look pretty good, don't they?" His question is rhetorical and the postman continues, "Yes, I imagine they take a lot of time, a lot of trouble."

"No," Anne assures him, wishing that he would go away so that she might open the letter, the letter which will bring the bits of her world together again —perhaps the most important piece of mail she will ever receive. She wishes passionately that he would go, but knows that every morning of her life she must always be pleasant, to the postman, the milkman, the laundry man, to a whole world of smiling people with so many "good mornings", so many little chats. "Oh, no," her voice is soft, lilting, "flowers are no trouble at all. I rather like to garden." Her head feels feverish and swollen suddenly, as though it were whirling about on its own. With an effort she focuses her eyes on the postman.

"Well they look pretty good." He turns away and digs into his leather pouch to sort out the next few letters but, Anne thinks happily that no one else's mail can have any importance; there is no other letter from Rosemary. She brushes the dirt from her fingers and reverently tears open the thin paper envelope.

She can have read only the first few sentences—it is a matter of seconds—when tears begin to roll down her fine, long cheeks. Awkwardly her body jerks forward and she weeps into the flowers, but there is no one to see or no one to guess that Anne Sedgely is not studying a leaf or a petal with botanical precision. Now her arms fall limp at her sides and in one hand the letter, partially read, dangles carelessly in the dirt. She gets up quickly and runs into the house.

In the front hall of Lane House it is cool, formal; four Lanes, two gentlemen and two ladies, are here depicted in the stiff poses of the traditional ancestor-portrait. Each one of them seems supremely satisfied with his own dark clothes, his own dull background and his own superior morality. Anne Sedgely clutches the newel post at the bottom of the stairs and looks, through a blur of tears, at the grandfather clock that tells her, stubbornly, inaccurately, that it is four-thirty.

"Good Lord," Mrs. McCabe appears at the head of the stairs dressed out in mops, filthy grey cleaning rags and a galvanized pail. "What's the matter with you, Mrs. Sedgely?"

Anne sniffs and dabs at her eyes. "Why, it's merely the flowers Mrs. McCabe, my same old allergy."

"Well your face is awful, like you been crying."
Mrs. McCabe bites off her comment with an assumed
harshness. "Your eyes are that red. Rip them up. I told
you that about the roses out back. Rip them up and
those in front too. What's the use, you suffering for
the look of things!"

"What, indeed," thought Anne Sedgely, "is the use
of suffering this way? Why not kick the hand-turned
newel post in anger, kick it and kick it until the wood
is dented, splintered and mottled black from my shoe.
Or tear at the bannister with my hands in desperation
and sorrow. The delicate spindles would snap like dry
twigs . . . why not destroy them, rip at them until my
flesh and nails split and the bones crack in my brittle
fingers? Why not indeed?" (She was still sniffing
slightly) "tear up the roses, tear up the red maple and
the border of pinks, tear it all up. There is obviously
no *use* at all."

Anne stood motionless at the bottom of the stairs
and looked up at Mrs. McCabe. "Would you mind
sorting out the towels in the linen closet, Mrs.
McCabe? I'm afraid I dumped things helter-skelter
when the laundry came back." It was irritating after
all these years, the way Mrs. McCabe had to be sent
from one chore to the next, constantly directed as
though she were a child.

The front door was still open and Anne went to shut
it. With the slightest touch of her hand the big oak
door swung closed against the June day. Still a bright
disc wavered before her eyes, as though a piece of
that exquisite sunlight from the lawn refused to be
shut out. It flitted, a dazzling particle, around the hall
—dancing up and down the staircase, settling now on
a heavy gold picture frame until at last with a final
sniff Anne blinked it out of existence and raised the
letter in her hand close to her red-rimmed eyes.

"Dearest Anne," the letter began. (It had come about quite naturally some years ago that Rosemary began to call her mother by her first name and Anne Sedgely had always considered this to be an indication of their frank and healthy relationship.)

Dearest Anne,

I am sorry that I have not written, but it is terribly embarrassing. I mean Daddy is perfectly fine but I hardly think that he is about to come home just now. His whole life is so utterly different.

He is in excellent health, very tan but a bit fat—I suppose from all the pasta. Really, except for a paunch in front he looks marvellous but of course so *different*, I mean his clothes and his manner might seem strange to you. He insists on wearing those deathly Italian shoes that are narrow and pointy. He has two pairs—one a shiny, black leather like patent-leather and the other light tan suede, rather yellowish, with little holes punched all over —too disgusting. Perhaps it is just because he is chubby that his suit seems tight. It is of a striped material, big stripes of black, grey, and white, and double-breasted—a style that Daddy never wore at home. Signor Popperatti, who is very friendly but kind of greasy, made it for him and says that it will last forever. Actually, I guess the Italians *like* sort of tight jackets and narrow trousers.

The point is that his clothes are so much a part of him and I am not sure that you could bear to see him so completely changed. He is very jolly and talks a great deal in Italian, and naturally I can only make out the simplest words. Really, I think you would understand, Anne, if you could see him promenade up and down the Corso Vanucci in the evenings—he seems to know everyone and is very much admired. It is incredible, especially the moustache; *that* is shocking! Daddy has an enormous white moustache with sharp ends—Garibaldi-shaped he says—and I suspect that he waxes the tips because there is always a strong smell of lavender—a sort of musty pomade smell whenever he is close-by.

I'm afraid that I disagree with you about the house. I think it is *divine,* though of course you are right, it is small. I sleep on a folding cot under the living room window because Daddy says it is "più fresca" which seems to mean that it is 99° instead of 102°. An old woman, Luisa, comes in to do the cleaning and cooking. Since I am at my Italian classes I don't see her too often, except that she stays to serve lunch sometimes. It is probably just as well because though she is very sweet she speaks terribly fast and being deaf could not hear me even if she could understand my Italian. Today she made some marvellous lasagna for lunch.

I can't recall that you ever mentioned Carlotta and Ennio Manzini who live next door. They both speak a little English—they learned it in the High School—Carlotta is thirtyish and *on the heavy side* as Mrs. McCabe would say—the pasta again. Though communication is desperate, I gather that the Manzini are sort of impoverished but a family that is quite important in Perugia. Both Carlotta and Ennio are awfully fond of Daddy and spend a great deal of time with him—and *time* they have as they don't seem to *do* much. Ennio is very dashing, black hair, dark eyes, etc. and takes me to the *Università* on his Lambretta—terrifying.

In the Italian class we are still on dreary conversations about books and pencils being on tables or in the hand. Daddy helps enormously with my Italian at home and I am *forced* to speak to the Manzini in the most embarrassing short sentences and have not yet found one occasion to mention a pencil being anywhere.

I am not sure that I see what you objected to in Perugia. I think it is marvellous, divinely medieval. The Duccio Madonna with the green face is perfection and I adore the Perugino Nativity and even the Fra Angelico which I suppose is a bit sentimental. In Daddy's garden there is a deathly statue of Christ which Carlotta gave him—too disgusting, with a pretty face and white night-gown. It is really impossible to understand how these people can be surrounded by such marvellous churches, frescoes, fountains, etc. and choose to live with these moulded plaster saints—I mean especially when one is from a good family.

Actually, I can't bear to write this letter to you after all we had hoped. Daddy is perhaps more entrenched here than we had imagined and he is so much admired, but most of all he is so utterly different that I think it might be terribly difficult for you to see him. Maybe I feel this way because I have only been here for one week and cannot possibly tell—I mean, Anne, that after all we decided I should not *plague* Daddy with questions or beg him to come home or anything like that. Please don't be upset—you have always been so marvellous about the whole mess.

Give my love to Will. Tell Braddy that I miss him (which is a lie) and I certainly hope he is walking again.

Much love,
Rosemary

P.S. There is a divine Persian in my Italian class who speaks with the most beautiful British accent

74

and I'm sure he must own a desert or an oil well as he drives the sexiest Alfa Romeo.

The night after Rosemary Sedgely had written and mailed the letter to her mother she sat on the edge of her folding cot in the Villa Carina and cried. She realized that writing that letter to Anne was the first thoroughly dishonest act of her life. "To write that stupid letter." She tortured herself by reconstructing the scene. It was after lunch and she tried to blame the letter on the wine—she wasn't used to all the wine yet. It was such a divine lunch, lasagna and then Carlotta and Ennio had come to visit. Daddy had been charming and gay and made them all laugh and then she had remembered about Anne and gone off by herself to write that hideous, lying letter.

"God it was hot in this room. The moonlight on the walls was more beautiful than sunlight but it only looked cool and blue, another deception. Wasn't it impossible though to write to your mother and say, 'Look, we've been fools. Your husband doesn't know you exist. He is a marvellous man, good-looking, spirited, divinely young. He doesn't care at all about the remote little people at home . . . He's so much more . . .' " Rosemary doubted seriously if life had to be that direct and honest.

Without a sob the tears ran down her thin face. In the still, hot night they mingled with the sweat on her long cheeks, forming larger drops that ran off her chin. Of course, it hadn't been all lies, not every word. Her father, *Signor Alberto*, was funny, really funny in his striped suit and Italian shoes, but his moustache was so grand, so debonair. He was wonderful, a dramatic figure : imposing, but not at all fat and certainly not laughable. She wondered if Anne would laugh when she read that ridiculous description of her husband— *bravo, molto bravo*, is what Carlotta said about him.

75

Wasn't it impossible though to write to Anne, who was so remote, so perfect in her own way, and make her understand that her husband raves in Italian, waves his arms about in delight after a good meal? Rosemary smiled, a wan, pitiful smile through the constant stream of tears—Daddy had been so charming after lunch, making them all laugh in two languages.

She twisted her thin head and looked out into the garden—silly to put her bed under the window when there was no breeze, only the moonlight that seemed less hot than the sun. Kneeling on the little bed her limbs were angular; the knees sharp, the elbows pointy. Rosemary, staring out into the dishevelled garden saw the Christ, a cheap plaster image, iridescent in the moonlight. That at least was true—she reaffirmed her report to Anne—he was disgusting with his holy brown curls, his holy pink cheeks. He never looked at her or at anyone, but concentrated always and everlastingly his holy blue eyes on the weeds and the dust.

God, it was much too hot. Oh why did she write that letter—too deathly—and say that Carlotta was fat? It was so untrue. Carlotta was all curves with lovely, black hair and big breasts—she was round in the stomach and the rear, lovely like a Rubens, fleshy and mature. In art class how she had disdained Rubens as decadent, frivolous—but she hadn't understood, felt the effect of the big sweeping canvases when they were cut down on a coloured slide and flashed on a screen to be sneered at. Carlotta was beautiful.

Unbuttoning the jacket of her pyjamas—they were fashioned like a boy's shirt—Rosemary looked down at her own flat breasts, so awful to have nothing there at all. The divine Persian would never notice her. She was elongated like a statue with a modern stretched quality, like Anne. In the moonlight she wondered, with the exaggerated bitterness of youth, if there was

76

a heart under the shallow left bump on her chest—like his, that dreary Christ, and if so, wasn't it bleeding those same red drops. She could almost feel the drops of blood, like tears—Rosemary raised her dampish hand to touch her own perspiring flesh. God, it must be a sin to be so dishonest and to write a letter like that to your own mother.

III

ELAINE GREEN WAS JUST ABOUT TO SHAMPOO HER LONG
blond hair. Earlier in the morning she had fought
with her husband about this very thing. No, it wasn't a
fight, Elaine decided, just one of their silly arguments.
To her it was extremely simple: she had such a busy
morning planned—pick up the house, bathe the
baby, an enormous wash to put in the machine, and
she just *had* to shampoo her hair. Obviously Phil
would have to go to the A. & P.—it was the only solu-
tion; but he had been nasty about it. "For Christ's
sake," he yelled, "how many times a week do you wash
your hair?"

Unnecessarily coarse, that's what Elaine thought, so
she had stopped right in the middle of opening the
frozen orange juice and gone to bathe little Sally.
"Well Philip Green"—she always used his full name
at times like this to let him know how angry she could
be—"I can remember—not very long ago—when you
were only too pleathed with my hair—nonthensical of
me, naive to think . . ." and then she laughed in that
aloof and sophisticated way and waltzed straight out
of the kitchen. Naturally she would not speak to him
after that—it was effective, Elaine thought, almost
speaking the words to herself, not to communicate
with a person when that person was being stubborn
and nasty. A silly argument, anyway, because in about
five minutes Phil admitted he was wrong—that is he
came into the bedroom and kissed Sally and kissed
her. "O.K., what do you want at the store? I suppose

78

not even God, my dear, could love you for yourself alone and not your yellow hair."

Phil was always saying crazy things like that. Three hours later it finally occurred to Elaine that after all her hair was a part of herself alone, wasn't it?—growing right out of her scalp, dripping now into the sink. She wrapped a bath towel around her head, but even veiled as a nun Elaine Green was beautiful.

The door bell chimed. "Just a minute," she called and slipped into a pale blue housecoat. "Carol, come on in. It ith you, Carol?"

Carol Perkins threw open the front door and lumbered into the living room. In her arms she lugged—as though she were carrying several heavy volumes—a white blanket stuffed with the figure of Samuel Perkins, Jr. The child whimpered.

"What'th the matter?" Elaine raised her lisping voice to a falsetto as she rushed towards the white bundle. The baby, not able to distinguish the features of her face, shrieked in fright at the approaching mass of light. "Yeth, yeth," she said soothingly, her lips pursed, "he's a lovely boy."

"It's too hot for the blanket," Carol reported in a matter-of-fact tone, "but Sam thought we had better keep it on him since we had not asked the doctor if we could take it off. Poor thing, he does cry so in the heat. But now you are inside," she reasoned to her infant son.

Elaine took the baby from his mother, unwrapped him, and set him amid the bright chintz roses on her couch. "We'll fix him a little plathe." She sang: "Here's a nithe little beddy." Together the two women smoothed the chintz slip-cover and gathered three or four rosy silk pillows to form a barricade around the small Samuel. It was an odd picture as they fussed over the baby: Elaine Green in her pastel wrapper was only twenty-three—she had a placid, girlish

79

face, her eyes were blue, her skin milky, and on her cheeks there was a natural glow which made her look the perfect young mother, the happy young woman in soap and baby oil advertisements. Carol Perkins, only forty, seemed much older than her age. Her grey hair was drawn tight into a school marm's knot and her face was wizened and mousy but with dark, intelligent eyes. It had become increasingly difficult for Carol to look at herself in the mirror. Three months ago, in April, she brought Samuel Perkins, Jr. into the world and today she might easily pass for the child's grandmother. Her eyes darted about the cluttered living room, but among the organdy ruffles, the teeny end tables, the cute porcelain vases and the prints of *La Mode Illustrée*, she discovered no sign of one year old Sally Green, "Where is Sally?" Carol Perkins demanded.

"Oh," Elaine drew her mouth into a childish pout. "She had a little trouble, thso I gave her an enema. Sally loveths that. It makes her thso happy, but thleepy too, my she's thleepy after her enema and I wanted to pick up, thso she's in her crib and I wanted to wash my hair too, thso after I called you . . ." Elaine disclosed everything, every event of her lively morning in minute detail. The milk had come late, but it was a perfect day for drying the clothes so Phil had to go to the A. & P. "He'th such a help."

"But he hasn't come home," she thought, "probably he's in that old library buried in some boring old history magazine while the frozen peas and butter melt and turn bad in the back of the car." She would have gone to the store herself if she didn't *have* to wash her hair. "It'th getting darker," she said to her friend, "and if I don't wath it all the time there would be practically no blonde left at all, and Phil would die if I uthed anything on it." Elaine drew a chair up to the sunniest window and shook her damp golden curls in the light. "He'th just crazy about my hair," she added.

"Heavens no, you shouldn't touch that lovely hair." Carol was in perfect agreement and though she had never devoted herself to hair-dos and fashions before the birth of her child, now she agreed that it was all very important. She was glad, in point of fact, that Elaine Green had introduced the subject into the morning's casual visit, because the week after little Sam was born Carol had gone through a frightening ordeal: she had looked at herself in a mirror, the first time in years. She was two days out of the hospital and feeling fine, as spry as when she began her dissertation fifteen years ago.

It was a painful moment to recall: pacing up and down the bedroom floor with the baby, she had suddenly looked at herself in the mirror—a little woman with a pinched face and her nothing-coloured hair all gone to grey—prematurely grey, of course, but she looked so old. And Carol Perkins wondered, did others look at her this way, as a remarkably plain woman bearing a first child in her fortieth year. Then, she had surveyed her face critically: it was small and sharp, but not yet lined, the dark eyes were lively still. Her hair was the problem, that dull grey head made her look so old, and drawn back into a tight knot it was not at all flattering. Never before had there been time or energy to waste on her appearance—the hours, the weeks, the years had been spent sorting out the argument of Russell, Wittgenstein, Ryle—why she had been devoted, almost religiously, to Russell in the barren years before little Samuel. And contemplating her own ugliness, Carol Perkins had kissed her baby and told him that philosophy wasn't everything, no, sweetums, she said, it wasn't the whole world.

What did others think of her, her friends and Sam's colleagues? Did they realize the merciless truth which the mirror reflected, that in ten years she would be fifty and her little boy still on his first bicycle. Carol had calculated that he would be in the fifth grade, and stated in such specific terms it seemed macabre indeed. If she had her hair cut ... a softer look, with maybe a few curls close to the face—she had read an article in the maternity ward in one of those foolish lady magazines about "filling out" a narrow face. Would it be too extreme, she had wondered, to have a rinse—an unobtrusive brown colour perhaps—or would she look ridiculous.

The baby was born on the twentieth of April, and for weeks (sixty-five days to be exact) Carol Perkins had been obsessed with the idea of dyeing her hair. She wanted to be transformed into a more attractive and appropriate mother, and she had studied herself innumerable times since that first shattering look in the mirror. She had arranged a mud-brown silk handkerchief about her face to simulate a head of short brunette curls. The effect was exhilarating to her—she *was* transformed.

After two weeks of worrying (the baby was then twenty-five days old), worrying about what Sam might think of her idea and posing again and again with the mud-brown handkerchief on her head, Carol had put it to him bluntly: "Sam, I'm thinking of getting a hair cut and maybe a little rinse."

Sam Perkins was reading A. J. Ayer in *Mind*. He did not look up at his wife but said, "Good."

Her mousy face was pained, "You were not listening to me."

"Why, yes, dear," indulgently he lowered the journal. "You're going to do something to your hair—that sounds fine. Smarten up a bit, eh?" And then with more sincere animation, Sam Perkins asked, "Say, have you seen this Ayer review yet. He may be old hat but he does it every time—cuts right through the nonsense." When Carol said that she had neither the time nor the inclination to read it, he returned to *Mind*, a little annoyed, for he had lost the line of argument, a demanding linguistic demonstration—momentarily destroyed—and besides Carol was behaving damn peculiarly of late. His thoughts did not turn at once to the book review: he speculated on post-partum depression.

Over a month had gone by and now Carol Perkins was delighted that her friend, Elaine, who was so experienced in these matters, had mentioned the subject of "touching up" one's hair. "No, you shouldn't do a thing to your beautiful hair, but you know . . ." Carol stopped abruptly not sure how to present her case. She was not used to sharing confidences with other ladies, but finally she plunged ahead. "I feel so much younger now that I have the baby. Frankly, I have been thinking of a rinse. At my age it might appear foolish . . ."

"Foolith!" Elaine Green screeched her protest. "Thertainly not." She thought it was a wonderful idea and Carol was absolutely right. Why everyone touched up her hair a bit—it was just like using lipstick.

"Do you really think so?" Carol Perkins was pleased and surprised.

"Of course, and it ith very attractive. Look at Anne Sedgely." They both agreed that Anne Sedgely must use a rinse on her hair. "Must have it done professionally though," Elaine said, "I mean I can't thee her taking any chances."

"Poor Anne." Carol sucked her cheeks in sadly and appeared more rodent-like than ever.

"Yeth, poor Mrs. Sedgely." They were both silent for a moment, a pause *in memoriam*. "How could he go off and leave her?" Elaine asked.

"Oh, he didn't leave her. He sent her away. One would never think of Albert Sedgely as a cruel man, but he sent her back all alone—and in a sense he did

leave their child." This last thought filled Carol Perkins with horror and she reached out to touch the baby
fuzz on her son's head, but little Samuel, sleeping
soundly, ignored the caress of her rough hand. "And
then for Anne to send her daughter off to Italy. I don't
understand—to be so alone."

"Well," Elaine said quite cheerily, "I just know I'd
be lotht without Phil, lotht, lotht." Her hair was
almost dry from the sun and she thought she might
warm up the breakfast coffee and take Sally out of her
crib.

"I don't understand the cruelty of that man, and
Anne Sedgely is such a bright, pretty woman. It is
strange," Carol said, "to know a man for a long time,
to grow more and more familiar with his mannerisms,
his foibles, the quality of his mind, and never realize—
Sam and Albert Sedgely worked together on the discipline committee for years—and never realize that
you were intimate with a mask, a brilliantly developed
persona that screened an irresponsible, selfish, probably very sick man capable of rejecting his child, I
don't understand." Carol wagged her mousy grey head
in despair.

Elaine agreed that she did not understand either
and went to reheat the coffee. The cups which she
brought out were in keeping with the décor of her
apartment—imitation Dresden with dainty, pink buds
sprinkled inside and out. Elaine gave one of the cups
to Carol and lowered her voice to a tone of solemn
intimacy reserved for her deepest observations. "You
know, Phil says that Mrs. Thedgely seems a very cold
perthon; but you know what I say." She paused, her
cup of stale coffee held dramatically in mid-air, "I thay
she is not a real human being." She turned quickly,
her angelic hair and her blue housecoat sweeping out
behind her in a final emphasis as she left the room to
go wake up Sally. The terminology Elaine Green had

thought out herself: people were either warm, "real human beings," or cold, "*not* real human beings." The system was uncomplicated: those who were involved with the basic and true business of life were real human beings. Those who always talked about art and politics and merely tolerated little Sally, the dull academicians of this college community, were *not* real human beings.

Elaine realized, of course, that she could be wrong about people. Until very recently she had thought that Carol Perkins was not a real human being, quite chilly with those beady, dark eyes. It just went to show how careful you had to be. Why since Samuel, Jr. was born Carol had become so interesting and pleasant. Elaine decided that there was a wonderful flowering in the older woman—they agreed on so many things now. Who would ever have thought that she and Carol would become such good friends? Oh, she could remember just last fall, the dry, little lady— a real mouse—talking on and on to Phil about the most boring things, existence and words, or the existence of words—something like that, *not* human.

"The's all warm from her little nap." Elaine returned with Sally, a blonde, doll-like creature of thirteen months.

"Sally, Sally! Oh, she looks just like you." Carol cooed this for the hundredth time. "Let me hold her." She took the chubby girl on her thin lapless thighs. Carol thought of the hours wasted on the assumption that p implies q, or given x equals y then—not to mention her critique of the problems of infinity. She bounced the baby girl up and down, up and down, and she was overcome with the bitter remembrance of all the years that had escaped her. She had been exactly like poor Anne Sedgely, never good-looking, but otherwise exactly like Anne—not a real human being. Elaine was so right. Up and down, up and down. Baby

Sally, as simple as her mother gurgled with delight.

"Wait, wait, wait," Elaine puckered her lips into three mock kisses for her little girl. "Wait till I get your daddy, thso bad in that nasty library . . . thso bad with those frothen peas and butter thawing in the car."

"Oh, dear," Carol Perkins pushed little Sally off her lap. There was a wet circle on her skirt. They all laughed—Sally laughed, the two mothers laughed, and Samuel Perkins, Jr. turning on the rosy silk pillows laughed a happy burp in his sleep.

In the beginning, when Albert Sedgely was left alone in Perugia, it seemed as though his very dreams had come true, as though the projection of himself which he had seen clearly in the Porta Marzia and the underground fortress could walk and talk, and what is more important feel. With Anne gone he could at last begin to act out his plans, and he was most successful. To start with he improved his Italian—ah, but not as Albert Sedgely might improve a language, with a grammar book and faithful attendance at the *Università*. The day after Anne went off to Rome he walked into town and sat at the most crowded café. There he smiled and nodded, and quite naturally, after three or four days of smiling and nodding, he became known. The Italians began to talk to him and he took an apéritif with the usual patrons. He listened, he imitated, and when he spoke he made up in his facial expression and gestures what he lacked in his speech. He discovered that he had a gift for mimicry, and an almost unconscious flair for the inflections and rhythms of the language. This was the only proper way to learn a foreign tongue, but you had to be prepared to make a fool of yourself, too—not an easy proposition for a learned man of fifty, but for Albert Sedgely it became easy. From time to time he would weaken and look up a few words in the dictionary or run over a verb construction in his mind. Within a month he was speaking rapidly, a bit ungrammatically but that seemed to make him more appealing to his Italian friends.

Perugia is a small city and soon Sedgely became a familiar figure, *il professore, l'Americano* who walked from his little villa up to the Corso Vanucci smiling and chatting with the people. He met Signor Popperatti, the best tailor in town who was also one of the leading Communists, and commissioned a striped suit in the Italian fashion. During each fitting Sedgely argued vehemently (it was great fun) against a narrow Stalinist view, and disregarding all sense of proportion, presented Popperatti—mouth unfairly full of pins—with a god-like portrait of Franklin Delano Roosevelt.

It was inevitable in such a small city that Sedgely would also come across his guide to the underground fortress, Luigi Rocetti. They bowed to each other in the cafés, and one day they were formally introduced. This second meeting with Rocetti was, though he did not know it, Sedgely's victory—he offered his hand and said how very much he had enjoyed the tour, and now that he was more permanent in Perugia he hoped that he might come again some day. Rocetti was amazed at Sedgely's fluency and charm and found the wooden, boring American quite a different person.

"Piacere, molto piacere," Sedgely said. He departed, imitating perfectly a formal Italian manner: *"Arrivederla, Signore."* The "r's" trilled like so many liquid ripples over his tongue.

Above all there was Carlotta. Sedgely's new suit and elegant manners were pale trappings, indeed, beside his affair with Carlotta Manzini: beautiful and lonely woman dressed in rags, she had come to life at Albert Sedgely's touch. Her history was so sad that she told it all to the kind *professore*, and he, moved nearly to tears, drew his own conclusions: her father, the villain in the piece, had been an inflated bore. Old Manzini (Carlotta canonized him) had started as a poor civil servant in the local *Fascisti*. In the confusion which followed Mussolini's attack on Ethiopia he was quickly advanced to a high ranking officer. At once the Manzini became the most pompous family in Perugia and Carlotta was sent off to a convent to be trained to the *hauteur* of the Italian nobility. She returned during the religious holidays and condescended to her former playmates, addressing them as *Signorino, Signorina*.

Carlotta Manzini grew into a beautiful young woman, but after the war the old families of Perugia would have nothing to do with the Manzini, and her father, by this time a *gran generale*, insisted that she was too good for any ordinary man. But now *Il Gran Generale* was dead, and in her poverty and pride she still greeted the *piccola borghesia* with a patronizing nod, and that was the end of it. It was generally assumed that she would never marry, and though she was now in her thirties and growing fleshy she was still addressed, out of a perverse Italian sense of delicacy, as *Signorina*.

For all her seeming pretension, Carlotta was a good and simple woman who held tight to her lying memories of better days; and to add to her unhappy lot she had a young brother, Ennio, who was a great burden. He was a handsome, athletic boy with no brains, and he too was tainted by the *Generale's* assumption that the Manzini were an important family. He would not work and he had neither the money nor the intelligence to take up a profession, so he became the local soccer and racing hero. He drove everything—a car, a motor scooter, even a bicycle—to its ultimate speed. And Carlotta, poor woman, would do anything for him. She loved Ennio beyond all reason and hoped against all the odds that he might still live up to her memory of their father, and several times a day she told him that old Manzini had been *bravo*, a man *molto bravo*.

On a warm evening in early April, Carlotta walked into town to find Ennio. He had come home a few days ago on a new Lambretta (she dared not ask where the machine came from) and had demanded money for gasoline. Since then she had not seen him. Worn out by her solitary vigil, she put on her frayed black suit—Carlotta mourned forever *Il Gran Generale*—and climbed a mile up the cobblestone streets in shoes that were worn thin to find her little brother. She walked up and down the Corso Vanucci twice but Ennio was nowhere in sight. She wandered back to the big café, hoping that among the groups of men she might catch a glimpse of him. As she picked her way among the tottery metal chairs she smiled and said her haughty, *"Buona sera,"* to the right and to the left. Ah, but it was degrading to ask after Ennio as though he were a common vagabond—she turned and saw Luigi Rocetti sitting with a foreign gentleman, some unsuspecting tourist he had picked up in the Porta Marzia Carlotta presumed. She thought that of all the people there Rocetti was the least significant; it could not matter what he thought of her, so she went up to him and said, *"Buona sera,"* and explained that she was to meet her brother, her brother Ennio, and that she was late, yes, late for the appointment and had Rocetti seen him.

No, Ennio had not been in the café that evening. Rocetti extended his stained yellow hand to Carlotta and said that he had much pleasure in introducing the American, a *professore*. Carlotta, too, had much pleasure, *"piacere, molto piacere,"* and when the American suggested that she have coffee with them how could she refuse the dignified *professore*, even if he was in the company of Luigi Rocetti. He was so gallant, so distinguished and she, Carlotta, was so tired from her walk into town. A hush of curiosity came over the café as Carlotta Manzini, the beautiful daughter of the big blown-up General, sat down in public for the first time.

The American was living here in Perugia—"*Ah, si,*" Sedgely said, "*veramente.*" He was living at the Villa Carina.

"*Dio. Dio,*" Carlotta cried, sounding not at all the proud daughter of an important fascist. Why that was the next house down from hers on the Via Venti Settembre.

After an espresso, Signor Alberto Sedgely and Signorina Manzini left the café together; after all they were going in the same direction. Rocetti, a picture of evil, picked at his nut-coloured teeth with a match and followed the jaunty figure of Sedgely, and the lush, womanly figure of Carlotta, with his squinty, dark eyes. It galled the wretched guide and he thought that his luck had all gone bad. For years Rocetti had been finished with his sour skinny wife, and his lustful eyes followed the pretty girls, all the pretty girls in town—but that Manzini woman, he said, she was the prize. Yes, it was a piece of rotten luck, his introducing them, but he said to himself that he might fool one, the American—he might act the cavalier, with his thin beginnings of a white moustache but he would never make it with a woman like Carlotta. It was all show.

Rocetti was wrong, for by the time summer came it was general information that the American professor had taken the beautiful Manzini woman as his mistress. They were in town together nearly every night: he in the fine striped suit that Popperatti had tailored for him, and she, no longer wearing dull black, dressed like a girl—in colourful jersies and skirts. The wives of Perugia wondered what the old bluff Manzini would have said about his daughter now; they wondered, too, what Sedgely's wife would say—the tall one, no meat on her bones, who had gone away—if she could see her husband strutting and spreading his plumage like a cock, strutting up and down the Corso with his lady. He was very much admired.

It seemed to Albert Sedgely that his dreams were more than possible. He read Carducci, Dante, D'Annunzio; skittered from one poet to the next. He felt that he had annihilated that part of him which made literature only a clever game, and now he ignored allegorical complexities, reading with pure joy of the multifoliate rose, with pure horror of eyes propped eternally open by hell's wires. His real triumph, of course, was Carlotta. *He* (Sedgely as prince) had brought her back to the world of the living —he went with her into the surrounding *campagna* carrying a basket of bread and cheese and a bottle of wine. One brilliantly lit day followed another, and the heat, the summer drought were unrelenting, but to Sedgely it was a dusty paradise. His skin turned brown, his moustache flourished and every day he thought to himself that it was right and in the scheme of things to eat and drink and to go to bed with Carlotta. He would think, even while he made love to her, that he was entitled now, traditionally, to caress her thick, black hair and to run his hand along her white, newly-discovered body with the excitement of a passionate lover.

But even then, in the beginning, once or twice there was a further yearning, that he might be free—he was not sure from what, perhaps it was from his own conscious mind which reminded him constantly of his success. "You're doing fine," it told him. "You're just right." It was irritating, Sedgely thought, like the

cheap tune that won't stop singing in your head—
"You're fine. You're doing fine."

And so the year passed, and now Rosemary Sedgely
comes to visit her father and again there is no water
in Perugia. Although the land is still green—for the
olive trees and the grape vines suck deep into the
earth trying to sustain life—the annual summer
drought has begun. The Commune di Perugia already
rations the low waters of Lago Trasimeno. An official
notice is posted on walls throughout the town de-
claring that in private homes the faucets can be open
only between six-thirty and seven in the morning. If
Albert Sedgely does not get up at six-thirty to fill the
tub, the sinks, the pots, and even the unused bidet,
there will be no water. Then Luisa, the deaf servant,
will have to trudge up and down the dusty road, half
a mile to the fountain, half a mile back with two wine
bottles and a pail. Luisa is old, a woman of seventy,
and Sedgely cannot bear to watch her trudging up
and down the hot road with the two wine bottles and
one pail with barely enough water to cook the pasta.
If the tub is full, Sedgely does not have to get up
each morning because it holds enough water for two
days—except for Rosemary, he thinks, and her inces-
sant baths. He pities her constant battle against the
dirt and heat for he has given in—the only possible
way to live through the Umbrian summer. He's told
his daughter that she can go to the Albergo Diurno
and have a shower for 200 lira, but she will not return
after one experience in the public baths. And so it is
because of Rosemary that he drags himself out of bed
at six-thirty every morning and stumbles into the small
bathroom attached to his bedroom. On this morning in
mid-July he has filled the sink and the bidet but the
pressure is so low that the water only dribbles into
the tub. With an audible sigh Albert Sedgely esti-

mates that it will take fifteen or twenty minutes at least. He sits on the green plastic toilet seat and stares at the tile floor, his head drooping down, down, his eyelids growing heavier and heavier until they close over the fixed blue eyes.

Some minutes go by and Albert jerks his head up, startled, but the tub is only three-quarters full. What an enormous bore this all is, and he nods to himself sagely: this is the comic-relief in the small tragedy of a dry season—waiting for a porcelain bath tub to fill up while sitting on a green marbleized plastic toilet seat, and all within the medieval walls. But for the Italians he knows that there is no dichotomy. They are proud of their gaudy modern fixtures, integral to the *bella figura*, and they have lived through this dry, earth-cracking heat all their lives. To Luisa, for example, it seems no hardship at all, panting up the parched road like a trained mule for a few bottles of water. For the old woman there is no sorrow in the summer drought. One day in September or October it will begin to rain. Luisa smiles and tells Sedgely in the monotonous voice of the deaf that the Communists say that they will build the new aqueduct, but the Fascists had said that too—and before them the priests and the kings. She will be dead anyway, Luisa says—"*l'acquedotto, quest'acquedotto là*—" and she points rudely to heaven. This was one of her great jokes and it made her laugh time and time again, although she could no longer hear her own story.

To know exactly what would happen and to be satisfied with her prediction of inevitable rain—no, Sedgely wasn't like Luisa. He was insisting on the variations of life. He was proving, wasn't he, the possibilities of himself—but nature was not co-operating.

He looks at his face in the early morning mirror: a face darkened by the sun, the pale hair grown thin in front, the temples pleasantly white, and over his mouth the bloom of a magnificent, white moustache. He has grown the moustache full and shapes it into two points, into two symmetrical, sharp ends which require constant clipping and waxing. It is a pity— Sedgely twirls these same ends thoughtfully—that he can't buy a moustache wax without a scent: that smell of cheap lavender directly under his nose at all times is nauseating. A bit disappointing, he thinks, to dislike his perfumed hair. Carlotta, as a matter of fact, sniffed at his upper lip and said the moustache was like a flower, *una calla*, a lily. No, it was not correct; as a self-styled sensualist Sedgely was sure of that, to play off the aesthetic pleasure which he took in the sharp-ended *baffi* against the sensibilities of his own nose. But in the hot weather the wax *did* go rancid rather soon.

The bath tub is full. Now, very quietly he will sneak into the kitchen and run some water into two or three of the large pots, but very quietly so that Rosemary will not wake up. Poor child, she could not possibly understand why her father is in Italy filling pots with water at six-forty-five in the morning.

Albert Sedgely is embarrassed and hurt by his daughter's behaviour. Except for that first afternoon when he came out to greet her in the garden (and kept her waiting, Sedgely remembers with shame), Rosemary hardly mentioned Anne or the events of Lane House. She was enjoying herself tremendously; learning Italian, riding about on the Lambretta with Ennio. With the single-minded intensity of youth she has fallen in love with Italy, with his run-down villa, with his friends, and above all with his new life. Sedgely is disheartened; his daughter approves of him too thoroughly. Certainly, he thinks, remembering the image of himself in the mirror, she must find it strange to see her own father so completely transformed. She should object, she should hate me—but, it occurs to him with horror, perhaps she is the new generation, the children trained to accept their backgrounds or their parents or whatever it is that used to get so neatly rejected—at least for a while—in the process of growing up. Perhaps his daughter is one of the aware young people exposed to Psychology 11 or 12, or whatever the number of the course; or it might be a smattering of sociology that had over-simplified their particular world into upper-middle, lower-middle, ethnic, educated groups. He finds it amusing to think of himself as a maladjusted, upper-middle, Anglo-Saxon Ph.D., and he imagines that it must be boring beyond measure to tolerate everyone, to understand, or feel that you *should* understand all sorts of dull people. Doesn't all that lead you finally to accept the injustices of the world, just as Luisa accepts this long summer drought?

To Albert Sedgely it seems impossible that a thin stream of water running into a big aluminium cooking pot could be so thunderous. He had stolen safely through the living room where Rosemary was sleeping in the morning sunlight, her narrow head turned out towards the garden. The water suddenly blasts, turned on full force at the waterworks—unnerving to him because right now before the day was properly started he does not want to talk to Rosemary. Oh, poor child, he is probably unjust to her. She is just a girl enjoying her summer vacation and in Europe at that, why shouldn't she adore it? Certainly he should be the last person to complain—it was a good deal more comfortable for him to have her happy. Still it *is* disappointing —Albert Sedgely tortures himself with the idea—because as part of his new existence it would be so appropriate to have a daughter who is angry with him, rebellious. He supposes he is aching for something more than the trumped-up violence of his political arguments with Popperatti. It is his fault, after all,

Sedgely decides, his and Anne's, that their child is at once girlishly enthusiastic and the cool young lady —no, their little girl could never say, "Daddy, I think you're a rotten old fool. Will you for Christ's sake come home," or "you filthy old lecher". She has been too well bred, too well bred even to have guessed the affair with Carlotta, too well bred to bring on a vulgar scene any more than Anne could, or, Sedgely admits regretfully, "than I could have a year ago— *Madonna, Madonna* isn't it odd to wish my own child would tell me to go to hell? Poor little girl."

The aluminium pot is nearly full and has become heavy. Uninterested in his simple chore, Sedgely does not hold it firmly and with a crash the pot drops into the sink.

Of course, the noise has awakened Rosemary. "Daddy, is that you?"

He is in despair. "Yes," Albert answers weakly.

"What's the matter?" Her voice is still thick with sleep. He can hear her getting out of bed to come to the kitchen.

"Nothing, I dropped a pot of water in the sink. Not a drop spilled."

"Oh," Rosemary leans against the doorway in her boyish pyjamas. "You're wonderful." She smiles at her father and Sedgely self-consciously reaches for another pot, clatters it about, clanks it in the sink, opens the faucet full to run the water.

"Daddy," Rosemary raises her voice, "do you hate me for being like mother?"

"Good Lord," Sedgely thinks, she can't be fully awake.

Here is Rosemary looking like an adolescent boy and asking me that incredible question, a question that is not censored, but carried into the daylight from her dreams. He pretends not to have heard— but at that moment the Commune di Perugia shuts the main valve and the faucet in Albert Sedgely's kitchen gives one final sputter and all is silent.

"Do you, Daddy?" the girl insists.

"Certainly not," and as he answers he thinks that his tone is a classroom tone—the professor explaining though never patronizing, "Why, it's very nice to be like your mother."

"But looking like Anne, I mean; doesn't it remind you all the time ..." Rosemary trails off, confused. She is aware now of every word and ashamed of her early-morning frankness.

"Yes, of course you remind me of Anne," he says kindly. He sees his daughter, a slim, straight figure leaning in the doorway and she *is* remarkably like her mother, though the body is too masculine, and the features of Anne are caricatured in Rosemary's sharp nose and elongated chin. At eighteen, Sedgely thinks, she is attractive—her cap of blonde hair and her youthful skin—though not pretty. She has the look of a young animal, a carved, mythical animal—she is physical enough but not bestial. It is a shame, really, because all of Anne's features are there on her face, but they come to a point, converge in—in a snout actually, like the snout of a narrow-headed dog. "You have the same splendid features as your mother," he tells her.

"Well," Rosemary smiles apologetically, "as long as I don't make you unhappy."

She turns to walk away, but Sedgely calls her back. An oppressive feeling of responsibility comes over him, a sensation of heaviness and heat that pushes against him, and he realizes that now he is obliged to talk to her. "I'm delighted that you're here with me, and of course you make me happy. You seem to be having such a good time."

"There now," he thinks to himself, "I've done it. I've been the dutiful father again for a moment and

97

perhaps it will be enough." And he says cheerily, "Let me make some coffee. It is much too hot to go back to sleep."

"I guess I'm like Anne, Daddy. I mean it's more than just looking like her." Damn the child, Sedgely thinks, she will go on. Well, he supposes it is unavoidable. It has to come some time, the "little talk" that seldom, as far as he is concerned, enlightens any situation.

". . . and I would rather," Rosemary continued, "be like you. But then I've been thinking it might be awful for you to have me around, that I might remind you of when you were unhappy with Anne."

"Now we have it." Sedgely is amazed at his own oversight. The easiest and most inadequate explanation of his prolonged visit in Italy has occurred to his daughter, and it strikes him as being particularly sad —any intelligent young person would naturally but unimaginatively (this was the discouraging part) think of "marital problems"—what an ugly phrase. "I was never unhappy with your mother," he replies, "just with myself. Anne has nothing to do with it. I'm sure I feel quite the same towards Anne."

"But you left her."

"In point of fact," Sedgely says pleasantly, "she left me, but again that has nothing to do with it. What I left—or what I am leaving constantly . . ." his words sound dry to him; whatever he will say to her will be partial, uninteresting, a synopsis, ". . . is what I was, my whole life."

"But I know," Rosemary's eyes are bright with admiration. "You want to live without all the nonsense —not just Anne, but all the awful academic types, the classes, the cocktail parties, our house even."

"No," he says it softly and Rosemary does not hear.

"When I remember, Daddy," she goes on, "how for-

98

mal and stiff you used to be—honestly, I know how boring it must have been."

"No, no," Sedgely feels he must correct her. "It wasn't boring at all. I was fascinated all my life by the problems of literature and of criticism. I did exactly as I wished; Anne and I lived contentedly enough. But I wanted to try something else. I always believed that some day I would be able to lead a different life if I chose." Sedgely sounds worn and old: it is not possible in this heat to put a buoyancy in his words, or to convey anything remotely like the freedom he had anticipated in his Italian life. "Coming to Europe should have been the perfect time to change; but you know, it wasn't. Anne and I were exactly the same, looking at pictures and churches in a perceptive way —knowing that Caravaggio was the best of the *sei cento*, or at least the most fashionable, and that Orvieto was a tolerable wine."

"But I do know," Rosemary looks at her father with dramatic intensity, "we are so horribly studied—so predictable, like that drooling dog. We are so dreary that after one art class I can't see a Fra Angelico without knowing it is a bit too sweet—it's deathly." She is excited now, and draws her thin hands together and separates them again in a gesture of applause, in complete approval of her father's performance. "But you *have* changed, Daddy, and you have all these new responses and everything. I think you are marvellous, just marvellous."

Yes, now she will romanticize my efforts, thinks Sedgely, but without wit, in a few pseudo-scientific terms incongruously sprinkled with youthful exuberance . . . ah, marvellous, deathly, dreary. "No, I'm not at all marvellous," he says to her, "I'm probably just a middle-aged man acting like an ass. Where does Luisa hide the coffee?"

He laughs because it is worthless trying to explain

to Rosemary. He was not thoroughly dissatisfied with the past, nor unhappy in his marriage. It was simply, he tells himself, that he believed he might of his own volition and desire make another world, a much larger world and it didn't have that quality of perfect bliss (he knew what the human being was born to) that Rosemary's immature vision would have. He wanted to take his life as it was and alter its limits as though he lived in a theatrical set, movable flats—and having created a new scene, then he could shift his tastes, his emotions, even his appearance. It was not easy, oh no, at this very moment he can feel the aches in his body from a hot and wakeful night. He got out of bed at six-thirty to fill the damn tub, and the moustache—unwaxed as yet—droops annoyingly over his mouth. But since Rosemary can not understand, it is best to make coffee, awaken her if only in a practical sense to the day at hand. The most he can do is love her, and that is in the scheme, so he reaches across the table and strokes her long hand.

"Daddy?" Rosemary asks dreamily, "can I invite Abdul Shah Amul to lunch?"

"Who?"

"Abdul Shah Amul," Rosemary repeats. "He is a Persian in my Italian class, really divine."

"An Iranian," Sedgely suggests.

"He says Persian, and he is giving me a ride home today." She blushes and cocks her head demurely.

"Of course, we shall have the Aga Khan if you want him for lunch," he says. And then he reminds her that last night they invited Ennio and Carlotta and Luisa has promised her best *risotto*, so they will have a wonderful party. "But isn't it strange," Albert Sedgely smiles to himself, "to have a daughter of eighteen? And isn't it excellent to know that she is not too predictable, not as yet?"

At twelve forty-five a vermilion Alfa Romeo blazed up the Via XX Settembre. With a purr it slithered to the side of the dusty road in front of Albert Sedgely's little house. In a state of over-excitement, Rosemary threw open the flaming door and gracelessly struggled out of the low car, catching her heel in the cockpit door frame.

Abdul Shah Amul unbuckled his safety belt: he was unruffled, meticulous in his Balliol blazer and light grey Daks. Slowly he walked around his svelte automobile and steadied Rosemary's tottery form as she wiggled her foot into the lost shoe. "Dreadfully sorry," he said. His British accent was ripe. "How beastly of me not to have helped you out." His apology implied that he thought it extraordinary for a lady to attempt to step out of a vehicle unassisted.

"*Niente*," Rosemary said with a shrill laugh.

They entered the house, and immediately from the inner coolness Albert Sedgely appeared and offered his hand to the dark young man. Bowing slightly from the waist, Abdul Shah Amul shook hands in the western fashion. His sleepy eyelids were raised languidly to take in the American gentleman and then relaxed over his black, marble eyes. "Awfully pleased," he said. "What a perfectly charming little 'villa'." With his tone he set aside "villa", subtly and inoffensively he imagined, to distinguish this badly redone farm house from the luxurious country houses of Italy.

They talked distantly to each other of the heat, and the Persian thought disdainfully that he had been tricked: could this be the father of Miss Sedgely, the cheery American girl? Abdul was particularly attracted by her blonde hair, the fairness of her complexion, and her tailored, almost English looks. Yet this aged man, her father, had *purposely* browned his skin in the sun and chosen to dress in the fashion of the Italian lower classes. He supposed that it might

101

be worse—only last weekend he had seen a group of tourists from the United States in pale green nylon shirts. He thought that Miss Sedgely was different— ah, what a pity that her father was this comic figure in cheap striped suiting. Unconsciously, he ran his fingers over the cashmere stuff of his own Balliol jacket.

"A very inadequate little house," Sedgely was saying. He put his arm around Rosemary and they walked the few steps to the living room. With his free hand he swept the air, "*Casa, mia, casa mia.*" The Italians, you know, *Signore*, do not have a word for home, but that does not mean they don't love their houses." He remembered suddenly that he had told his daughter this same bit that awkward day of her arrival. "On the contrary," he continued, "the meanest little shack is a *palazzo* in sentiment."

"There is no lack of sentiment in this country," the Persian agreed.

"Daddy, Abdul Shah Amul is going to study architecture in Rome when our Italian course is finished," Rosemary said, but she needn't have changed the subject for at that moment a cry of terror, a screech of brakes announced Carlotta and Ennio on the Lambretta. They burst into the house, kissing Rosemary, kissing Sedgely, and screaming at each other.

Ennio had nearly killed her, Carlotta said, on that machine—"*pazzo, pazzo.*" Well she would rather cook herself to death walking on the road than ride with this crazy-boy again. Ennio swaggered his narrow hips, all too well displayed in his blue jeans (*tipo-Americano*) and gave a childish imitation of an angry Carlotta. There was a sudden pause—Abdul Shah Amul had stepped into a dark corner to observe the peculiarities of this uncontrolled greeting.

"Forgive me," Rosemary said, lunging towards the Persian. She was conscious of her ungainliness—she, the perfectly trained young lady, stumbling out of cars, ignoring her guest, but he was so terribly inscrutable and so divinely attractive, this black-eyed young man with the reserved British manner. "Perhaps," she thought, "I should have asked Daddy to wear an American suit just this once, but then Ennio has on those obscene blue jeans and Carlotta's pink jersey blouse is so absolutely *stretched* over her great breasts." In her memorized Italian phrases she introduced Abdul Shah Amul to Ennio and Carlotta Manzini. The Persian was pleased to meet the friends of Signorina Sedgely and he bowed over Carlotta's hand —not touching it but formally addressing his heavy-lidded eyes to the rough skin on the back of her fingers.

Then Ennio asked how fast could the Alfa Romeo go and the party settled down to their steaming rice. Sedgely poured out a good deal of red wine. It became obvious after the first few minutes that Abdul was unable to understand Ennio's rapid, colloquial speech. They had finished a simple discussion of how fast one could travel to Rome, to Florence, to Bologna, on a Lambretta and how many litres of gasoline the Alfa Romeo used per kilometre. In the circumstances Abdul imagined his limited ability in the language to be an advantage and Ennio happily turned to Sedgely and his sister to report the morning's gossip from the Corso Vanucci. Rosemary was left to her Arab.

"What does this man do?" Abdul Shah Amul asked about Ennio with complete indifference.

"I don't understand exactly what he does. He goes into town most of the time and sits at the cafés. Sometimes he races, professionally you know—cars and motor scooters." Rosemary looked across the table at handsome, stupid Ennio gabbling on. It occurred to her for the first time that he really was worthless. "Then he plays soccer with the local team. I think he's awfully good. Last year a man from Milan almost hired

Ennio for their big team. They talk about it in town all the time."

"Mmmm, interesting. Good show," the Persian said distractedly.

"Wine, wine!" Albert Sedgely offered the *fiasco* around the table, but his daughter and her friend Abdul were not listening. " 'Wine, wine, wine'—the poet says. 'Another and yet another cup to drown the memory of this impertinence.' "

Abdul Shah Amul raised an eyelid, "The poet?"

"Omar," Sedgely replied and was about to go on but Rosemary said, "Daddy!"

Graciously he attended to Carlotta and Ennio—all three of them had another glass. "What fraud," Sedgely thought, "an Anglophile Arab in his Harrow tie and Balliol blazer and Rosemary loving it, ignoring Ennio and Carlotta and eating every morsel of Mr. Shah's greasy chips and watery marrow." For the second time that day the obvious was revealed to him—it was like Rosemary's idea that he and Anne had been incompatible—the easiest notion which somehow never entered into his complex machinations—and he realized that *he* might be seen merely as an Italophile: *Signor Alberto*, a shallow expatriate-type, a diverting ape, who dressed, talked, ate Italian. The notion infuriated him.

Ennio said that Popperatti was having *mal di fegato* this morning and could not drink his coffee. Carlotta tossed her wild black hair, raised her striking head and said—just finishing the rich pasta course and her third glass of wine—she too had *mal di fegato*, that she could eat nothing, nothing. Ennio reported two German ladies in at the Brufani Palace, very ugly, and a smart looking couple, Swedes, with a car he had never seen before. He wondered how fast it would go.

"Baroque," said Abdul Shah Amul to Rosemary, "is not to be overlooked. The earliest stuff, Bernini, Boromini is quite acceptable, but the really excellent, full-blown and I dare say, much superior Baroque, is in Vienna."

"I *adore* Viennese Baroque." She closed her eyes in rapture; unfortunately she could not recall a coloured slide or the name of any particular church from Art II.

"The difficulty is that you can not have a nave," he went on, "a central nave—which after all elongates the structure, tends to lengthen and arch the line—and a dome at the same time. It simply never works." What else, thought Abdul Shah Amul, was he to say to this pathetic Miss Sedgely? The effort of talking to that Italian racer was painful, and he did not wish to go any further with the mad professor, or Carlotta whom he presumed to be his mistress—and a good thing she looked too. Abdul ignored a platter of grey veal cutlets that Luisa offered under his nose. "Sitwell, don't you think, is delightful on Baroque."

"Yes," Rosemary pretended, "awfully good."

"Saint Peter's, for instance, is a terrible mistake. The conflict between dome and nave are almost irreconcilable. One will always be unhappy walking into that church until one stands under the dome directly; otherwise it is most unsettling."

Albert Sedgely listened closely to his daughter and her Persian friend. It was a poor scene for him to watch: Rosemary tagging after a dusky Anglophile who had picked up the effete conversational tricks of Oxford, with none of the immense knowledge that gives wit to a smart phrase. And you could tell, Sedgely thought, that he had salvaged these chatty gems from some long forgotten tea-time discussion, and is presenting them now—random second-hand thoughts—to Rosemary who hasn't the vaguest idea how to play his game. Furthermore, Sedgely swallowed down a glass of wine in disgust; furthermore, the audacity of this popinjay to speak of feeling in a church. Why, my simple, childlike Carlotta can feel in Santa Maria del Popolo, the most egregiously decorated, the most offensively designed church in all of Umbria. He teetered towards Carlotta and patted her plump thigh, "unsettling walking into St. Peter's" indeed, Mr. Shah—and Rosemary barking after him like a puppy—poor little girl, probably thinks he means the Sitwell in a turban.

"Here, here," Sedgely interrupted a lecture on the optical illusions in baroque arches. "You must have more wine. This is very good Chianti."

"Thanks awfully, but I haven't finished," said Abdul decisively.

"No, thank you, Daddy." Rosemary shook her head stiffly, suggesting that quite enough wine had been drunk already. Sedgely poured a glass for himself and a glass for Carlotta, who was devouring her second veal cutlet and recalling the stature of the *Gran Generale*—his height, his breadth, and how he had suffered bravely in the liver as well as in the kidneys. Ennio drew soccer plays into the tablecloth with his knife and made motor noises with his mouth.

"I'm sorry," Rosemary turned to the Persian, "you were saying?"

"Yes, about St. Peter's, awfully unsettling that, don't you think?"

Rosemary had never seen St. Peter's, but she said, "I *loathe* St. Peter's." She was sure that Abdul was perfectly right, but she wondered secretly if St. Peter's had to be unsettling and though Anne and Daddy had brought her up without any religious nonsense at all she supposed that old women and nuns might feel absolutely ecstatic in St. Peter's. She remembered that Mrs. McCabe had gone to Rome with her sodality during the Holy Year and had cried when she saw all that carved marble and gold—it was so gorgeous. But

naturally it didn't matter about Mrs. McCabe's crying
—it couldn't possibly, any more than it mattered what
Carlotta said about the most exquisite madonna: that
the face was sweet, the hair pretty, the baby beautiful.
She wondered what religious sect Abdul belonged to
and thought that next year she would take a course
in comparative religion. "But your mosques," she said
tentatively. "How could you look at our little domes
after your mosques?"

"Good show. You may have hit it. Exactly why I
can't abide them, except of course . . ."

"I've just uncorked this bottle," Sedgely shouted,
waving the straw-bound flask, splashing the wine over
the white cloth. His eyes were blood-shot and a
smudge of tomato sauce streaked his moustache. "But
you must have some. You can't spoil a good party."

"Thanks awfully." Abdul Shah Amul suffered his
glass to be filled a second time.

"No thank you, Daddy."

"Carlotta," Sedgely crooned, *"la più bella, sempre e
dovunque . . ."*

"Except of course," the princely face, darker and
more withdrawn, turned once again with an Asiatic
endurance of the ages to talk to his hostess, "St. Paul's.
It is a perfect church."

"I adore St. Paul's." She gazed at him—how exciting
his skin was, a mellow brown, his hair so black with
coal-blue lights and his perfect, sharp-cut nose and
cruel mouth. Rosemary could see him, a mirage, in
the towel-like head-dress of a sheikh with a multicoloured blanket pinned about him—though, of
course, he was divine in his Balliol blazer, too. She
hadn't known what college it was, but had asked him
after class one day. "Are you a Mohammedan?" she
asked now, "I'm dreadfully bad on religion."

"Anglican," he replied crisply.

"Signore, signore," Carlotta presented her large

breasts and like La Maja Vestida, she seemed more seductive in the pink jersey blouse which merely suggested clothing than if she had been nude. Very slowly Carlotta spoke the English sentence she had been working out in her mind, "He ess like my Valentino, no?"

"Perfect! He's the sheikh," cried Sedgely. He saw his daughter staring wide-eyed at him. "Ah yes, of course, she is surely my daughter and the daughter of Anne, and right at this moment," thought Sedgely, "it is a simple matter of being furious with the old man for getting drunk. Oh, glum and moral Miss, I can never escape the fact that you are mine. I am condemned, for all my supposed freedom, to watch you blush at the sight of your father and . . . and furthermore a very decided and conditioning furthermore, to love you . . . and to know that even if I could not hear you and if you were not with me now in Italy, I would be conscious of you, though I could not hear your words— you and Anne would go on like some dumb show, far-off, but always and always in the recesses of my mind." Albert Sedgely drank another glass of wine and told himself that he certainly didn't care what this damn darky prince thought, because *he* thought it was about time if he was to be any kind of success at all. It was just the right time, so he said very rudely : "I suppose, Mr. Amul—how does one address you, I mean properly, in the British Isles?"

"Shah Amul," he answered curtly and withdrew under thick lids.

"I suppose you have oil wells out there in the desert?"

"There are fortunate pipe lines which run through my father's kingdom."

"Shah Amul is going to study architecture in Rome after our summer course." Rosemary's thin face was distorted with anxiety. Her father was being awful, behaving like a beery Irishman, and Carlotta in that revolting pink, nearly flesh-coloured jersey, offering herself around the table. "It is too disgusting, and haven't *I* been the fool," thought Rosemary, "taken in by all her constant talk of the Virgin and saints and that foul plaster statue in the garden. She is ugly, really ugly with that fat, vulgar shape. Christ, how terrible of me to invite Shah Amul. How deathly of me to bring him to this cramped little house and to my father and his degrading friends. Yet only this morning," Rosemary reminded herself, "I loved it all so very much; then, before I *knew*—it was too revolting, Carlotta and my father, and oh, God, look at Ennio batting grape seeds up and down the table with a tooth-pick." In that moment Rosemary felt that she was duped by time because what she had felt early in the morning was so long ago that she could not remember and what she felt now was immediate, permanent: "I *do* feel different," she assured herself, "utterly, utterly different."

"*Benissimo*," Albert Sedgely sang out, "Oil like liquid gold coursing through the desert. Golden blood coursing through your veins. This wine," he continued irrelevantly, filling his glass with the strong red Chianti, "is very, very good. The intake of liquid is extremely important, especially in this heat . . . I suppose, being from the desert Mr. Abdul we make you feel quite at home here in Perugia." With marked courtesy Sedgely turned to Carlotta and Ennio and translated his remarks into Italian.

In desperation Rosemary said, "I think the museum here is nicely done."

"Rather," said Shah Amul, refusing an apple.

"I adore the Duccio Crucifix," she said flatly.

"I think you will find that crucifix is Maestro de San Francesco. Yes, it's amazing, the effect of dead flesh on wood."

Five grape seeds were drawn up for the champion roll: Ennio giggled with joy and smoothed the table cloth to keep them in line. Her father's hand, Rosemary noticed, was deep in the black tangled curls of Carlotta's hair, and he leaned forward to whisper something to her, very close, very intimate—he tickled her soft olive cheek with his moustache. He fondled a gold ring in her ear with the tip of his finger.

"Dear God, he is repulsive." Rosemary tried to look away. The litter of fruit cores, seeds, crusts and the wine stains on the table cloth formed a tattery *collage* —the ruins of a meal. A rind of gorgonzola encrusted with mould was folded into her father's napkin. Rosemary Sedgely was upset, an acid, sour feeling in her throat, her head throbbing, and that watering in the mouth as though she were about to be car-sick, but here she was, not going anywhere, not likely to go anywhere—as a matter of fact she had the sensation of having arrived again, this was—she remembered the term—a *déjà vu,* but having arrived where? Familiar and yet unknown—it was not this table but the garden outside . . . "and the time must be the day I arrived at my father's house—the same confusion, disorder and the stomach-turning heat. It is sickening enough that he has insulted Shah Amul, but it's excruciating, this display with Carlotta. He is being physical with her, *physical.*" And it crossed Rosemary's mind for the first time, as a truly new idea, that this naturally was not the first time for them. He was honestly a revolting old man, deathly—and her marvellous Oxford Arabian must be revolted too. "Wouldn't Anne die, simply die, to think of Daddy as a lecherous old man? Yes, he was old, a fanny pincher and a drunk besides."

"So," Albert Sedgely drew himself up into a rigid pose of decorum and asked pompously, "You are going to be an architect, are you?"

"Yes."

"What sort of thing do they build in Iran?"

"My father would first like a hotel in Teheran." Shah Amul replied as politely as possible.

"Won't that be fine," thought Sedgely, "just fine! A miniature of St. Paul's sitting on a sand pile, but naturally it will be bigger—enormous—make St. Paul's look like a pigeon-stained bird house." He smiled indulgently: "Well, well, a pleasure dome."

Abdul Shah Amul returned the smile mechanically and looked at his watch, "Very too bad," he rose from the table—"It is frightfully late."

Everyone stood and there was much handshaking, "*Arrivederla*" said over and over again. Ennio complimented Shah Amul for a final time on the beauty of his car. He came round the table, swaggering in his tight blue jeans, his pelvis tilted forward so that it drew the rest of his athletic body after, and he looked with a boyish, beguiling smile at the Persian. He would like some day to ride in the car.

Rosemary led Shah Amul to the front door and he offered his hand to her as a matter of form. "Thanks awfully," he said repressing a yawn. "Good show."

"That man Sedgely was a professor in America," Abdul Shah Amul thought as he sped down the Via XX Settembre. "Why, they wouldn't let him char at Balliol." What incredible good fortune that he had not matriculated at Harvard!

Seated again at the lunch table, it occurred to Albert Sedgely that Luisa had not yet served the *dolce*. He had ordered it specially because it was Rosemary's favourite. Too bad, he would like to have seen that arrogant son-of-a-bitch eating *zuppa inglese*, but perfect touches like that are so seldom attained in real life. It was a thin and sloppy scene then, after all.

IV

WINTER IS HALF THE YEAR IN NORTHERN NEW ENGLAND. Before winter begins, and it begins too soon, autumn is dramatic, unbelievable every year—trees golden and orange-red, hay-coloured fields, sun and cider—all blazing in a brief, passionate death. But then long after snow, after freezing, the winter persists, rudely ignores the calendar, melting down from the mountains, swelling up through layers of soil, turning whole valleys to mud, shapeless and brown. In April it is still winter (dates are meaningless), but now like a gigantic lingering puddle it resists greenness and growth until the people, almost tasting the slop-brown earth, come to hate with a personal hate every leafless black branch in the sky. Encaged, taunted by the weather they dream ferociously of freedom, of breaking out of stale rooms into a world of colour and heat.

Like captive animals, the stir-crazed, barn-soured people turn mad in their fantasies. The sedentary clerk envisions himself swinging clubs, bats, rackets, until every muscle in his soft white body aches. Staring from the office window at a wet monochrome view, he would gladly martyr himself to the sun. And adolescent girls, bored with their woollens and school books, costume entire scenes on sun-drenched beaches, invent mauve gardens with romantic phonographs. On a bleak April afternoon, a girl of sixteen can picture the scarlet of her unbought bathing suit; can even hum the song she will dance to in June. Weary mothers endure, praying as they watch their pale sluggish children whine and crayon another magazine, that they will soon, dear Lord, very soon, be put out to pasture.

In Northern New England the winter is too long, and the summer cannot fulfil the dream-desired world of a non-existent spring. And desires are too tightly wound—once set off nothing stops them: stretching his first hit the clerk twists his ankle sliding into second base. The young girl sits on the front stoop suffering from sunburn—and alone in the moonlight, without music, she is painfully unkissed. The small child (in answer to his mother's prayers) plays out of door, driving his tricycle over and over the flower bed, or gobbling up the bitter red berries off the thorny bush. Each one seems to be unfortunately drawn to his opposite self and imagines a holiday role that is unfitting. And the ordinary, inoffensive people, are distorted during their brief summer vacations into pathetic, grotesque figures.

The academic community in which Anne Sedgely lives entertains itself throughout the long winter with art, literature, and politics reflected in cocktail party gossip or after dinner conversation, but at the end of the season, when it *should* be spring—on those dreariest, soggiest days, here the people dream, to be specific, of picnics. The professor who in a well-heated living room enjoys a glass of cognac coddled in the palm of his hand imagines that he would be happier with a can of slightly warm beer. The hostess envied for her *coq au vin* and Limoges believes during the season of dreams that she would actually prefer to serve hot dogs on a paper plate. A picnic, a carefree evening or a lazy afternoon becomes the particular hope; to speak of the *fête champêtre* becomes the vogue. In April and early May almost everyone says, "It won't be long now. We'll be having a picnic," or, "God, won't it be good to get out on Berry Hill?"

The faculty have nothing in common with Marie

113

Antoinette who with her gilded pail played milkmaid in the quaintness of the Petit Trianon. They are exceptionally plain and unpretentious people who genuinely feel that what they need is a bit of simple bucolic living—a rustic experience. Aside from the shameless, those with private incomes, there is not one member of the faculty who can afford a plaid-lined, thermos-fitted, leather-strapped picnic basket from Abercrombie's. But then, there are not many who when summer really comes attempt to fulfil the spring desires: perhaps it is self-knowledge, rationale, control, or old fashioned propriety, a summer picnic is unheard of in the town.

Elaine Green, however, was young and ideas stole quite without her noticing into her lovely head—but having stolen in they did not escape easily. She dwelt on, examined, judged her ideas and usually, for want of an argument or an alternative, she accepted rather than rejected them. Though often contradictory, these thoughts formed a cosy, comfortable and extremely tangible world for Elaine. A good way to entertain (this was one of her ideas) was to give a small supper party: a casserole, with garlic bread and salad, served buffet style because their apartment was so small that you couldn't get more than four people at the teeny drop leaf table—nasty. But now (this was a new thought) in the heat of summer, on a starry evening, a picnic would be so different and such fun. "Everyone alwayth talks about picnicking—but no one theemed to *do* it," Elaine said over the telephone with a persuasive smile.

"Yes?" Carol Perkins on her end of the line was unsure.

"Well," Elaine was almost belligerent, "I'm going to. I'm going to have a picnic."

"Yes?"

"Yeth—and just invite everyone and go *way* out and

114

everyone should bring something, don't you think, becauthe ith more fun that way?"

"Mm, yes ..." Carol was still doubtful. Across the room her pink, cherubic baby slept tranquilly on his rubberized sheet: he was so brave, so raw from the prickly heat. "Yes, Elaine," (there was courage in Carol Perkins' reply) "but *we* can't possibly come. I couldn't leave the baby, and if I did get a baby sitter I would hardly be able to telephone in from Berry Hill, would I?" There was no answer, so Carol continued, speaking into the mouthpiece, mingling gaiety with self-sacrifice. "But you go ahead. It does sound like fun."

"I haven't told Phil yet or anyone. It was my, my ..." Elaine trailed off in disappointment.

Samuel Perkins, Jr. beat his fists ineffectually against the muggy atmosphere. "The weather is so changeable," Carol said. "Well, I'd just be too nervous if we *deserted* him."

"I suppose it could rain," Elaine sighed.

Poor little Elaine, Carol thought, sweet and helpful, but still so young. She merely wanted an evening out, away from the house; why when her baby was as old as Sally Green, she supposed—though it was difficult to imagine now—that she would want to get out once in a while too. "I'll tell you, Elaine, you come over to our house and we'll have a charcoal fire in the back yard."

"Yeth?"

"Yes," Carol said definitely. She stared at the baby with nervous, black eyes. "But not too many people because the yard is small. I'll make hamburgers."

"Yeth!" The new thought had crept into Elaine's pretty blonde head and was taking hold. She was almost cheered. "I'll make my potato salad."

"Fine!" It seemed to Carol that little Sam was spottier than usual.

"And it will be motht informal," Elaine Green said. She had just bought a pair of flamingo toreador pants, bright cotton which clung to every curve of her youthful haunches. "You know, jutht old thlacks," she suggested to Carol.

"Yes." They both agreed.

Carol Perkins was thrilled that she could please her friend *and* sacrifice for her child. Elaine didn't mind having her plans cut down—it would have been such a battle with Phil to have a picnic. He could be stuffy and unreasonable about the tiniest things, but now she could wear her new red trousers anyway. "Wonderful," she chirped. "We'll have a cook-out."

"A cook-out, exactly." Before Carol Perkins had her baby she would have winced at the term, one of those awful tags out of the *Ladies' Home Journal*, but now as little Samuel writhed in the heat, she recalled reading an article just the other night, a very informative piece about the necessary adjustment in marriage to the arrival of a first child.

When Anne Sedgely was invited to a "cook-out", an evening of hamburgers and beer, she said: "It sounds delightful. The best kind of party."

Each summer in July she and Albert had always spent what they called "the haphazard month" in Maine, during which they cooked nearly everything on a charcoal fire. It really made her blue to remember because "the haphazard month" always proved such a rewarding vacation: to sleep late and wear old clothes, to lie in the sun and eat out of doors at irregular hours. In recent years Albert had not brought a scrap of work with him but just abandoned himself to the luxury of reading in his field. Except for the year of Rosemary's birth and the two or three summers they had been able to afford Europe, the Sedgelys

116

went to Maine every July for the relaxation and informality they so needed.

Anne Sedgely knew that Albert had loved Maine, too—the rented, draughty cottages on the coast, the long evenings with lobster or a thick steak turned on the fire and served with a chilled white wine or perhaps a good *rosé*. They usually finished the bottle between them and went to bed drowsy, heady. And she remembered Albert building a fire: he was remarkably skilled and sure. "It's odd," Anne thought, "I never knew where he had learned that trick, but he did it perfectly and like everything he turned his hand to, with knowledge." Those were fine evenings—whatever else he may have pretended in Lane House about their lives, whatever else he might be escaping from now, Anne was sure that he had loved those comfortable, silent dinners in Maine. So for her, the invitation to hamburgers and beer in the Perkins' back yard was delightful. It would recall that camping atmosphere, would be a touch of the old "haphazard month" that had always worked such miracles. One careless, therapeutic evening, she imagined, would be just the thing.

On the morning of the party Mrs. McCabe pressed Anne's grey linen bermuda shorts. She wore these with her madras jacket and a starched white shirt and assumed a casual air as she sauntered into the Perkins' small back yard. "I thought I'd better not ring," she said lightly. In her hands she balanced one of the Lane wedgwood platters with her contribution to the party enveloped in layers of waxed paper.

The yard, confined on one side by high unclipped bushes and on the other by the rear of the house, was the size of a small living room. Crowded with ten guests, canvas chairs, and card tables, it gave Anne the feeling of being cramped indoors. The guests, except for Will Aldrich who seemed to be tending the bar on the back porch, were all young instructors and

117

their wives. She supposed that Sam and Carol Perkins, rejuvenated by the birth of their son, had joined this younger set—but that was unfair, she told herself; it was not that they had given up their old friends, it was only the younger faculty who were financially forced to stay in town during the summer. Sam Perkins—his grey hair was going white she noticed—rose to greet her.

"I had better do something with this," Anne said, steadying the platter, "I'm afraid it's perishable."

Elaine Green, her hair drawn back into a single golden braid, her young form stuffed into her new flamingo trousers, rushed out of the back door and ran down the steps. With the tight pants she wore a white ruffled blouse, the whole costume made her look an improbable matador, blonde and defenceless. "What ith it?" Elaine screamed with excitement to know what Anne Sedgely had brought. Two or three young women gathered about the platter on which the Escoffier masterpiece, a resplendent *Rhum Mousse au Chocolat* was moulded into a creamy brown star.

"A *mousse*," Anne answered simply. "I thought it would be cool."

The *Rhum Mousse* was Anne Sedgely's best dessert and she was glad as she listened to the chorus of ohs and ahs that she had spent most of her afternoon creating it. In the growing dark of evening the chocolate star did not look its best, the colour seemed drab and the intricate design did not show up as it did by candlelight.

Not noticing colours or shapes, but quick with a standard reaction, Elaine cried: "Oh beautiful, thso beautiful. But it lookths too good to eat. I'll put it in the refrigerator."

Freed of her *mousse*, Anne stepped gingerly through the jumble on the lawn : legs, glasses, blankets

118

and bags of "fritos" and pretzels. Will Aldrich handed her a gin and tonic mixed exactly as she liked—very little gin.

"No golf this afternoon?" he asked.

"I'm sorry, Will, did you wait for me?" It was an offhanded apology—but after all these years they were such close friends that all their arrangements, especially their golfing arrangements were informal. Will Aldrich and Anne Sedgely played together almost every afternoon, but it was understood that if something sticky came up in the Dean's Office she would play with someone else, or, if something came up for Anne—say a *Rhum Mousse au Chocolat*— Will would find another partner. Anne moved away from him to be pleasant to the young wives, to ask about their children whose names and ages she carefully recalled.

Sy Jacobs, a brilliant economist and the current *enfant terrible* of the faculty, began to organize the fire-building. "We're all too fucking civilized . . ." he said loudly. Sy cultivated his coarseness as if it were a Harvard accent. ". . . Not one of us fat-heads can build a fire."

"No," Will Aldrich admitted, consciously playing the straight man, "and I hope I'm too intelligent to try."

"That's just it, damn it," Sy cursed on—charming, aggressive, tasteless. "Well, somebody with guts should try one *hell* of a fire, make a goddamn fool of himself and set the whole house blazing."

Anne Sedgely settled into a wobbly sling chair, listening passively to the talk. She watched Philip Green drag a large bag of charcoal across the lawn. He was the prototype of a serious young man—thin, dark, intense—he had already published a book (very well thought of) on Disraeli's Colonial Policy. Anne wondered, as she watched him touch a match to the un-

119

tidy pile of sticks and crumbled newspapers, where-ever had he found pretty, stupid Elaine? And what did they have to say to one another on an ordinary Wednesday morning? Not much, Anne suspected, because it was general information that Phil Green was buried in the library—a very hard-working young man everyone said—*his* book was not a revised dissertation. It was peculiar the way circumstances twisted the world about, Anne decided—peculiar to think that such an unsuitable match, the fragile blonde doll and the bright young scholar, would probably be the making of his career. Hidden away in the library, far from the lisping chatter and the organdy curtains, he would no doubt become a productive, first-rate historian.

"For Chrissake!" Sy Jacobs yowled down at Phil Green, who bent, bewildered, over the blazing newspaper. Full of good nature, Sy picked the *Times Book Review* out of the pile of old papers and began, ineffectively but vigorously, to fan the flames. "This is the lousiest fire I've ever seen," he said and the burning paper rapidly died into flaky ashes.

The evening shadows converged into a violet haze. There was no greenness left in the yard. The bushes and grass were indigo now, and Anne Sedgely detached herself—further than her age and loneliness detached her from these animated people—to watch the last streak of vermilion stretch into a thin line against the horizon, and fade to yellow behind the purple hills—"*tramonto*," she remembered from her Italian lessons, "behind, amidst, among the mountains." But it was so quick, this sunset, swallowed by the New England hills into night, an extreme and subtle beauty, while the sunsets in Italy, looking out from the nasty little garden at the Villa Carina, had seemed too theatrical—the sense of timing was off in those Perugia sunsets, even in the winter months. It was all too long and violent a dying, overdone like death in Verdi, the colours in vulgar kodachrome.

The talk washed about Anne in indistinguishable waves of words and phrases. She had not been listening, and she knew, turning to the dark figures near her that she must listen—given the fact that she was here in the Perkins' back yard at a party it was her responsibility. The shrill lisp of Elaine Green rose above the even hum of conversation. She was tilting her golden head sadly over the dead fire, pouting at her husband "Well, we are all ready," and "I don't thsee why you can't make a fire," she whined.

"Let me try it," Anne Sedgely said with enthusiasm. The back door slammed and she noticed, only for an instant, that Carol Perkins was coming towards her guests with pounds and pounds of raw hamburger patties. What is it, thought Anne, that seems odd about Carol tonight? It was difficult to see in the darkness —only the strange silhouette of her head, why it looked bloated, swollen. "Let me try a fire," Anne repeated. She had watched Albert so many times in Maine: his flames were always steady. And just as Albert had done during the "haphazard month", she first crumbled a bed of newspapers and then methodically constructed a network of sticks into a delicately balanced tepee—twig upon twig with room enough for air.

"Such precision," a voice behind her said. At exactly the correct moment Anne added the charcoal; she remembered that Albert had always preferred the manufactured briquets, but in spite of this her fire was a great success. "Now, she said, "I think we wait a while until the big flames die out."

Will Aldrich passed another round of drinks. As usual, she thought; this will be like so many ruined dinners, that extra martini to remove what she considered the fine edge of control.

Anne sat down on the grass and noticed again that something was different, rather strange about Carol Perkins' head. The pale, molelike face was unchanged, but the hair—that was it, the hair was dark and puffy. "I don't see very well at night," Anne said to a pregnant young woman, "has Carol cut her hair?"

"Isn't it lovely, Mrs. Sedgely?" the girl answered Anne with respect. "Carol has had a permanent. It's so young looking."

"Yes, lovely," Anne replied. In the firelight she could see by the quick orange flashes that Carol Perkins' hair was a harsh black, dyed to the lustre of coal. It was arranged in an elaborate pouf of curls which made her whole head, as Anne had first observed, seem disproportionately large for her wiry little body. On her narrow forehead a row of girlish bangs drooped to her eyes, pinched the burrowing face—the unnaturally dark hair accentuating her black animal eyes. "But how ghastly," Anne said to herself. "It brings out every line in her face, makes her ancient—like a shrivelled Navaho of ninety without one grey hair."

She smiled pleasantly as Carol Perkins came to join them. "Why we were just remarking how pretty your new hairdo is."

And then from the pregnant girl: "Lovely, I keep telling her how successful the tint is. I think you're silly, Carol, to need reassurance."

Nervously, Carol Perkins ran her bony fingers through the mass of absurdly pitch-coloured hair. "Oh, it's been almost a week now," she said apologetically to Anne. "Sam was annoyed at first, but I think he's coming round."

Five days ago when she had come home from the beauty-shop, Samuel Perkins had looked with bulging, furious eyes at his wife and told her she looked like a whore. For the next two days he had softened his criticism—"street-walker"—but yesterday and today he had said nothing, that is he had only asked with a stiff, paralytic twist to his mouth if she could comb some of that stuff out of her eyes. The entire beauty-shop experience was painful to Carol: once there, amid the chemical odours and unfamiliar potions, unguents, and plastic devices, she had panicked, and the permanent, the hair tinting, seemed utterly beyond her control. Frightened, over a copy of *Harper's Bazaar* with pictures of shadowy young people editing (in the rain on Montparnasse) *The Paris Review,* she thought only of little Samuel left alone with a high school girl, a hired nurse-maid she had met only momentarily. The afternoon of her permanent had the cruel reality of a dream episode, the hot air blowing into her brain—she could not hear no matter how urgent or frenzied the screams of her baby—and she comforted herself with ontological proofs, imperfectly remembered.

She was doubtful still about the colour: had never expected it to be quite so black, and the permanent seemed frizzy. Her friends, however, the young mothers in town who knew so much more about these things, all said that it was just fine and would be much softer after the first shampoo. Now, Anne Sedgely, whose taste was undisputed, had complimented her. "The switch on my bottle warmer ..." Carol could bear no further discussion of her new hair style, " ... seems to be broken and I'm lost without it."

"Oh, take mine," Elaine Green cried. "Thally has outgrown it."

"Can't you put the bottle in a pan of water and heat it?" Anne Sedgely suggested. Eighteen years ago, she recalled, she had managed very nicely with a sauce-pan on the stove.

"A bottle warmer is so exact," said the expectant mother.

"Yes, everything is scientific now. But then I'm old." Anne said without malice, "I go back to the pre-Spock days."

"Pre-Gesell," Carol Perkins corrected her.

Now they have started, Anne Sedgely told herself, and they will go on about formulas, schedules, and strained spinach. She did not resent being the middle-aged woman removed from the problems of bottle sanitation. Eighteen years ago she had brought Rosemary into the world and bred her with a minimum of fuss and bother—she had bathed and fed a daughter whom she loved quite as much as these ladies loved their children. It had bored her then to discuss diaper bleaches, and now, with Rosemary in college, nearly a grown woman, it was hardly more appealing. She was safe in the darkness to withdraw again . . . oh, to sit planted in the group, but as a remote body.

No one could see her torturing the lapel of her gay madras jacket with nervous fingers. Not one young mother could discern that her soft, lonely eyes were not focused on any object in the Perkins' yard. And it was better, Anne decided, not to feign an interest though she did it so well, because someone always discovered the effort that lay behind her casual remarks, or at least she *felt* that someone must realize that she was unconcerned, which was really just as trying for her. Naturally, she had never openly refused to exchange recipes, or conduct the futile personal surveys of soap powders and hand lotions. When, precisely when, Anne wondered, had she exiled herself from the talk of these women? Surely it was more than eighteen years ago. It must be her lifetime, forty-five years. She had been born apart from the petty businesses of life and she could not, no matter how she tried, make them take on importance. As a child in Lane House she had been surrounded by Georgian brick, old paintings, copper lustre, leather volumes, and a good deal of culture that was priggish and out-dated, to be sure. It never occurred to Anne Lane Sedgely to make the secrets of her ablutions or the process of her digestion topics of conversation. It was not that washing and eating were common or improper, but on this level, the humourless, house-wife talk, they were dull—a picking over of the minutia of life.

Anne snapped her cigarette case open—it was a thin silver case—and as she offered it in an unconscious gesture to the women about her, there were the usual compliments followed by an examination of the Florentine workmanship. She was amused listening to them now, for her simple gesture might have been contrived, like a literary convention—an object, a slim cigarette case given them for motivation—the ladies were turned about completely. The plot might wander on. Things became possible again, or impossible.

"I just don't have time to polish the silver," one woman said.

"But it'th worth it to me," Elaine Green stated her aesthetic principle.

"Well, I can't imagine it. After I've put in two loads of washing, made the beds, vacuumed, I can't imagine shining up the silver. When something special comes up I resurrect the wedding presents . . ."

Anne laughed with the audience, predicting to herself that the conversation would not be about Rennaissance goblets, the sale at Parke-Bernet, or even early American pewter moulds. No, she knew that at best they would end up with silver patterns, the advertised "Rose Lace", "Contour," "Queen Anne"; the uninherited, unhallmarked. heirlooms — tarnished forks, spoons, knives black with the oxide of disuse. In their earnest tedium of begetting, feeding, cleaning, the silverware was brought out for a visiting mother-in-law or the League of Women Voters. "You are probably right," Anne Sedgely said to the woman, and repeated it to herself, "They *are* right." All the while she had been twisting the imported bleeding madras of her lapel—perfectly ridiculous this—to be so ill at ease. She got up from the sling chair and said, "I'll do the hamburgers."

It was a relief to get away from the group of women. That was another bad sign to Anne—all the ladies together, all the men droning on, professionally, perhaps intelligently among themselves. She felt so incredibly alone, contemplating the raw beef. All by herself in the darkness, with so many people crowded into the small back yard and only the white coals visible on a bed of red heat. "It is one of those strange, isolated moments," Anne Sedgely thought, "when I am conscious only of a few details, the barbaric bloody flesh of beef, the fire and the night itself, hot and weighty in the air about me."

"Will, come help me," Anne called. Will Aldrich turned away from the cluster of young men. A tall, familiar figure, he came to her and together they put the hamburgers on a small grate over the fire. It was the second grade chopped meat from the supermarket and the fat spit up from the coals. In an effort to fulfil their roles of host and hostess, Sam and Carol Perkins stood helplessly by—but a cry, the enraged voice of Samuel, Jr. rang out across the yard and with terrified faces they both dashed into the house.

"And what do you think of the fright wig?" Will asked.

"Please, Will!" Anne made an amused shushing noise. He stood above the fire, turning the hamburgers, and his face seemed to Anne diabolical—that was the way faces always seemed, even the kindest, least cruel faces when lighted from below. Will Aldrich laughing gently at Carol Perkins was a genial, play-acting devil, like a child grimacing with a flashlight held under his chin. Softly, Anne said, "She is like one of those jet black Indian heads with the wizened face ... like the oldest head-hunter in the *National Geographic*."

"Yes, terrifying."

"Isn't it sad what people will do to themselves?" Anne said, and then ingenuously, because Will Aldrich was her one great friend whom she could ask any question, "Why, I wonder, don't people know what they want to be?"

"They know, Anne, that they don't want to be themselves. I suppose that for all the philosophical articles, or *because* of them, that is just where Carol is most stupid and most susceptible."

"How she looks?"

"Yes, of course," Will said. "Not an attractive picture to see yourself as a mousy old woman while you rock the new-born babe."

"Poor thing." Anne took the hamburgers that were done off the fire and began to split some rolls. "Well then," she whispered, "what about Elaine and the Spanish pants? Tell me what Elaine doesn't want to be."

"Isn't she wonderful, all that blond hair? But you would pick out the one exception to my theory. Elaine is so much on the surface, so beautifully uncomplicated that she can only want to be herself—so feminine and naturally sexy. Yes, the bright red pants are perfect." Will Aldrich smiled, and apart from the effective lighting, he consciously played at being evil, and made an appreciative noise with his mouth.

It annoyed Anne that anyone—but especially Will —anyone with a mind, anyone with sensitivity, would find Elaine appealing. "I think she is vulgar," Anne said, "because she doesn't have the foggiest notion in her wooden, dummy head what she suggests. Oh, she knows she's gorgeous, but then again she is the innocent, devoted mother and she would be shocked, truly shocked, if somebody took her up. She offers everything and gives nothing and, well ..." Anne faltered, embarrassed to be speaking this way, even if it was to Will Aldrich, ". . . well, there's a phrase for that sort of thing."

"My dear Anne," Will was amazed. "There is indeed a phrase for Elaine Green, but now you're the vulgar one, I'm happy to say."

There was an inefficient passing of plates and opening of beer cans. Sy Jacobs cursed the ketchup bottle. There was much shuffling, settling, re-settling—husbands and wives moved together again. Anne talked golf scores for a while and then listened graciously while Philip Green described the bibliographical problem in his latest article.

The gin and beer on such a hot summer evening had oppressed the party, and a drowsiness came over the campers: the talk died and the crickets' sharp cry dominated the stuffy little yard with nervous insistence. There was no interest in dessert. A pan of brownies made from a prepared mix and Anne Sedgely's Escoffier *mousse* were set side by side on a card table. Both delicacies were too rich, for the hot night and the brownies hardened while the *Rhum Mousse au Chocolat*, the precisely moulded star, melted into a semi-liquid. A few people spooned it, slopping the creamy chocolate onto their paper plates, but only the pregnant woman swayed heavily to the table for a second portion.

Anne Sedgely and Will Aldrich sat together on the Perkins' back stoop. The close summer air was thick with disappointment; Anne lit a cigarette and began nervously to tug at her lapel again. The mock picnic, the little "cook-out" had not worked for her, and looking about at the lumpish bodies squatting on the lawn, she doubted if it was a success for anyone. Sy Jacobs continued to be boisterous, about foreign aid now, and Anne felt that his unlovely manner was charming only during a brief interview. Carol, her puffed and dyed hair growing frizzier, bumbled up and down the steps, in and out the back door, to minister to the baby. Little Elaine—Anne could just catch a glimpse of her —pulled vacantly at her bright gold braid, her beauty and the toreador pants hidden by the night; she sat docile behind her husband who was lecturing tediously on the events leading up to the Sepoy Rebellion, more often referred to, he said, as the Indian Mutiny of 1857.

Anne was sure that if Albert had been present her evening would have been much livelier. For one thing, she now behaved differently, quite badly at times, ever since returning from Italy. Really, parties—even badly organized parties with tasteless food and dull people —used to be somewhat enjoyable, and the trivia of women's talk which she had always found boring had never annoyed her as it did tonight. She knew very well that it was not the absence of her husband's love that turned the Perkins' "cook-out" into a melancholy affair, for that touched only her innermost pride. It was the absence of Albert as he presented himself to the world. He could manipulate people beautifully towards a good conversation; he insisted that his friends be lively, and he had a wonderful technique, Anne remembered, for lightening a ponderous discussion by a clever and pertinent reference to the latest *New Yorker*. The gaiety she had so poorly pretended this evening would have been natural if Albert had been here, and certainly she would not have been nervous. Now Anne stopped tugging at her lapel and stamped out her cigarette. What a rotten, rotten party, she thought—and it occurred to her that perhaps she appeared lonely—perhaps she had been invited to be cheered. "I think I'll go home," she said to Will.

"You can't. It's too early," he put his hand out to hold her back. "We are expected to stay for a while around the old camp fire."

"It's practically burned out."

"If you go now you'll be rude."

"No I won't, because they don't think I can be." It was insufferable to be so edgy: she was beginning to argue with Will. Anne excused herself from the party.

Sam Perkins, as host, said: "I'm sorry, Anne, you can't stay."

"I am, too," she said, convincingly, "but I've had an overdose of golf today and then I gardened this morning. The flowers, you know, they irritate my eyes; but it was a lovely evening."

Everyone was sympathetic then and no one, except Will Aldrich, guessed that Anne had not played golf that day or that roses only irritated her eyes for less than a week at the end of May. She walked off without thanking Carol Perkins, who was in the house once more, feeling the hot, motionless air to make sure there was not a perverse current over the crib of her sweltering infant son.

Later Will knew how she felt, though he had guessed it on his own. She had gone home, Anne told him, and the stillness in the high hallway was almost as maddening as the chattering people and crickets she had left. In the Perkins' back yard she had been detached, but then in her empty house the loneliness crowded about her. The ceiling stretched white and cool, high above the entrance hall and staircase, the moulded ceiling with a border of garlands strung between clusters of grapes, and a clean, sweeping oval of leaves in the centre. But she didn't see it. Anne looked up at the detailed plaster-work (not Georgian, but disturbingly Federalist)

130

which she pointed out to visitors, and saw nothing of its beauty. She was limp, as Will had imagined her, from the evening of pretence and disappointment, alone in her hallway, staring up but not wanting to climb the good-example staircase to her silent bedroom—and what alternative?—She could turn the few steps into the living room where no chair was disarranged, where each satin pillow was carefully fluffed. For what? Sit on a couch. Do what?—Touch some ornament with her fingers in a useless way.

Will came up the front path, up to the door and rapped with the brass knocker, the original knocker designed for Lane House.

She heard a metallic rapping, a sharp unfamiliar noise, "Who's there?" Her voice, on the other side of the door, sounded tight to him, strained.

"Will," and he rapped sharply again with the knocker.

But naturally everyone used the doorbell, and the only time she had heard a tap from the knocker in years was when Mrs. McCabe polished the hardware —it frightened her. "Come in." Anne still looked frightened as she opened the door. "I'm jumpy tonight. Isn't it stupid? I'll soon be on drugs if my nerves keep up."

They went into the kitchen together and Anne got out two glasses. "Weren't you rude to leave so soon after I did?" she asked.

"It didn't matter. The whole thing was about to collapse and the fire did go out." She left him then, Will remembered, and he could hear her going about the house from room to room, pulling back the curtains, opening windows.

"It's cooler in here," she called. Will went and stood beside her at a front window. "I sleep on the couch some nights."

Later she told him she felt nothing unusual—only

131

a sense of pleasure to begin with—pleasure because she was not in the house alone. They looked out at the clipped lawn and the empty street. In the moonlight the border of pink flowers appeared gentian and the grass was an unearthly turquoise. Finally, when Anne spoke, he thought her words had a false ring, as though she had said them all to herself first: "Did I tell you? ... I must have forgotten. A letter came from Rosemary the other day."

He did not answer but put his hand to his forehead, pretended he was thinking, so that nothing would break through to him. Doesn't she find it odd, Will wondered, that I never mention them—Albert and Rosemary who should be as much a part of my life as anyone? Couldn't she see a difference all through the spring when I refused to answer? Can't she tell that I'm no good now as the *confidant*?

"This light," Anne said to him, "makes your hair silver instead of white."

"Changing the subject," Will thought, "but not for long. We always come back to it."

And she thought: "It's damn peculiar. He acts as though Albert had walked off the edge of the earth and Rosemary had followed after. This isn't fair—I have to recall them from the past, bring them awkwardly into the conversation so that they seem like ghostly figures. But he must understand. He spends all of his waking hours, and God only knows how many of what should be his sleeping hours with the problems of adolescent boys—acneed, sweaty-palmed youths who come to him as strangers." Anne realized it was bitter and foolish to think this way, because the traditional line on Will Aldrich was true: he was the towering, father-god, sympathetic, beyond measure, hero of all the students. "And granted," she argued with herself, "granted his own life is austere, celibate,

132

mysterious, whatever the tradition says, a life sacrificed to the undergraduate psyche—all that admitted, still to find that I, too, must come as those boys come —expose myself as helpless, tortured . . ." It was asking too much. It was unfair.

Later on Anne told him that he had seemed as inanimate as an idol, not answering, and she could not imagine what he had to offer her from all his supposed humanity and wisdom, perhaps no more than a relaxing game of golf or the security of a shared joke about Elaine Green. It was all very well for him to avoid the painful subject, she thought, but it made her situation no less painful; now that she had sent Rosemary off to Italy, Will was the only one she had. "You needn't be so careful with me," Anne said out loud, "and when we are hardly polite about so many things. Anyway," she continued, tapping his arm to make sure she had his attention, "it was a funny letter. I forget that Rosemary is so young, because I've treated her like an adult for so many years; and then, as I should have expected, she sends me a parody of a schoolgirl's letter."

"She is a little shocked," Will said.

"Yes."

"A little thrilled—in love with everything."

"Exactly." Anne began to laugh. Suddenly, it seemed like a joke—that Will should know precisely what it was about Rosemary's letter that was funny. "And she uses the same words over and over again." Anne Sedgely was laughing without restraint, and Will Aldrich stood immobile, with an indication of a smile on his face, staring out at the turquoise lawn. Anne was laughing about it for the first time since the beginning of all her difficulties with Albert, since the first subdued argument in their hotel room in Perugia. Until this moment it had all been so serious, leaving Albert in Italy, sending Rosemary off, the continual pretence in town, and her own ambiguous status as the loving wife, the lonely wife who had deserted. She saw at last that it had all been too serious, too heavy, and gasping for breath she mocked Rosemary's boarding school accent: "She writes the same *dreary* words over and over: *divine, marvellous, disgusting, too revolting.*"

Will Aldrich had no desire to dissect Anne's family problems with her newly discovered twist of humour. In the routine of his job he heard too many intimate confessions and saw too many hearts bared, the flexible hearts of young men stripped for his vision alone, to be interested in Anne's self-revelation, which would really not be a revelation to him. He knew, for she had told him so often, every word that Albert had said to her in Italy and what she had sensibly replied—and he felt, though he had never been there, that he knew the colour of the stones in the medieval wall, and the mood, the desolate winter mood of the damp and rundown villa in Perugia. He pictured some things without ever being told: Anne, drifting through the Roman ruins alone, selling the Fiat at a good price, then buying one return ticket to America—Anne, in dark travelling clothes, walking stiffly up the gangplank to a single cabin. He envisioned two people knowing everything and nothing about each other, caught in the meaningless years of marriage, house, job.

At that moment Will did not want to see her face (he thought her beautiful when she was laughing), not while she laughed at her daughter, at her husband. His head ablaze in the moonlight, hair wrought of precious metal, he still looked out onto the lawn as though something of infinite interest lay before him in the transfiguring light. "Poor Carol Perkins," he said at last, "what a shame. We shouldn't laugh at her."

"*I* shouldn't," Anne said. "I've been touching up the

grey in my hair for four years. But it works for me."
She felt relieved saying this because she had never
admitted it before. Oh, Albert and Rosemary knew
that she went to the beauty shop to have a rinse, but
the fact of it was so familiar that she had ceased to
think of her appointments—the scheduled Friday
afternoons when her head soaked in a purple-brown
liquid—as anything more than a part of the ritual of
her life. It never occurred to her that this hair tinting
was a deception; but having told Will Aldrich about
it she was buoyant, giddy. She wondered if this was
the sensation of a patient in analysis who stumbles
upon some part of his part, "Ah, yes, and I killed a
little sister when I was two—an accident . . ." or "One
day my uncle, he was fat and ugly . . ." and then remembers some dreadful obscenity, some sordid ride
on which everything hinges. Anne had this sense of
having told Will the first significant fact about herself,
and she continued, "Yes, I *dye* my hair, and shall I
tell you about my face creams? I'm wild right now
about hormones . . ."

"No, please. See out there," Will Aldrich said pointing to the lawn, "the grass is playing at being blue: it
has changed without any explanation. I don't want to
know why—light refractions, gaseous matter on the
moon." He held her throat—long and lovely—and
combed her hair roughly with his fingers, over and
over until it stood wild, savage to look on.

"Yes," Anne told him. "Yes." They were perfect,
one with another, natural. Here was her other existence, thrilling, sensual—she hadn't guessed. Their
bodies breathing together—she hadn't known, and
flaming through, welding them was her heart. She
loved him so completely.

When dawn came Will woke her, with a touch, and
he can remember her reaching up to him, long white
hollows in her body as her arms stretched up.

"The world is different now," she said, sticking out her chin like Rosemary's, *"marvellous, divine."*

Mrs. McCabe found two rings stained into the window sill from their glasses, but Anne didn't care a damn.

V

THE DAYS CONTINUED FOR ROSEMARY AND THE HOT
Italian nights passed as they had before she invited
Abdul Shah Amul to lunch in her father's house, so
that the first lesson which she learned—something she
could not have believed a short while before—was
that life—washing and eating and talking—goes on.
Her nights were restless, but her days, externally at
least, were quite the same at July's end as they had
been at the beginning of her Italian summer. In the
mornings she rode to school with Ennio, straddling
the back seat of his motor scooter, clutching his belt or
the back of his shirt as they raced to the *Università*.
Then she would smile and thank him and walk up
the worn stone steps into the cool, resounding palazzo.

The building which houses the University for Foreigners in Perugia is a luxurious seventeenth-century
palazzo that has been toned down into calm hallways
and well-planned classrooms. The reconstruction has
successfully turned the baroque palace into a school,
and even with the artful gold flourishes preserved on
doors and ceilings, even with carved tables and throne-
like chairs planted in corridors, there is the
empty, impersonal atmosphere of an institution. For
Rosemary Sedgely the morning hours which she spent
at the *Università* were the best hours of the day. Then
she was completely absorbed and she was glad that
her lessons were strictly confined to grammar and
pronunciation. If she were studying literature or art
she realized that her concentration might have been
imperfect, for given a poem or a picture her mind

137

wandered easily to a time in the past, and everything past was painful, and what seemed worse, she imagined the future and everything future to be more painful still.

Surrounded by a class of over fifty students, she repeated the memorized Italian sentences. They spoke out loud and in chorus to hear themselves speaking the unfamiliar words and to listen to their own phonetic blunders. The lessons were a simple mechanical process and Rosemary was thankful for them. Over and over she said, "*Io sto bene ma mio fratello è ammalato.*" She had no brother, never would have; it was so impossible and wonderfully remote from any of the facts which crowded about her during the rest of the day.

". . . *Ha la febbre e un forte mal di capo,*" she replied to her teacher, not caring in the least about this brother, his temperature or his headache. It was all so divinely abstract. How long has he been in bed?

She aped the words and the accent, "*Da tre giorni.*" Her Italian advanced rapidly.

After classes Rosemary would walk up the steep medieval street that led from the *Università* to the main piazza, and often she would find herself in a group of students with Abdul Shah Amul, or she would turn to find him seated at the next table in the big café. They always met in public and talked to each other in a frivolous way, as though nothing out of the ordinary had happened to them. He was excessively pleasant to her, and since he deigned to speak with only three or four of the students, she presumed that she was privileged. Her heart sank when he drove off alone in the beautiful scarlet car : she was feverish when he entered the classroom, but these symptoms had nothing to do with love, for she had never come close to him; perhaps it was her infatuation with a mythical sheikh and the disappointment that there was no possible role for her in this tale of Arabian nights. Her sickness was that he, Abdul Shah Amul, knew about the disgrace, her father and Carlotta Manzini, but she went no further than this in her acknowledgment because all the words that came to her mind seemed more appalling than the fact of Carlotta and her father. "Lover," "affair," "mistress," . . . disgusting words, but her discovery, unstated, cut deep into her at all times, every hour of the day and night—except during those mindless hours of the morning when she repeated the Italian sentences, *"Il mio fratello è ammalato."* Suspending shame and sin for three hours, Rosemary was free; drugged with verb tenses and vocabulary, she transferred her pain with great relief to the brother she would never have.

When Rosemary remembered the hateful luncheon the only thing which remained clear was a single gesture of her father; he put his arm around Carlotta, who in the flesh pink jersey had looked worse than naked, and his hand stroked her, resting familiarly on her heavy back. The very hand of her father that had been officially extended and warm by design—it moved up the fleshy back of Carlotta Manzini, who could have been, after all, his daughter—stroking up and up her back, caressing at last the nape of her neck, and finally that hand, she could see it, buried in the wilderness of Carlotta's black hair.

That was all Rosemary visualized, an isolated picture of Sedgely's hand upon Carlotta. Nothing else, not the wine or conversation, the food, or the insult of the meal had shape or form in her memory. But many other scenes which had been confusing and unclear now came into sharp focus. The day of her arrival when she sat outside in the hot garden waiting for her father to appear was no longer a mystery. Old Luisa had been frightened and upset, sent out into the yard to delay her. In her anger and shame Rosemary's interpretation became a bit more dramatic and a good deal more sordid than the facts allowed. It was obvious to the girl that she had been duped, led around to the back of the house while sheets and clothes were rearranged, while Carlotta slipped out the front door so she, the daughter, could enter into the farce. It was the classic *comédie*, like those farcical entanglements of Molière which she had struggled through line by line in French class : someone hidden behind the arras, under the table, in the draperies. To Rosemary the humour of the situation was outdated and rotten—not what her Persian would call a "good show" : and the dumb Luisa had appeared between the acts like a mime; she had danced a little *divertimento* while the scenery was shifted about.

This theatrical conception of her father's deceitful behaviour with Carlotta did not come to Rosemary at once. It developed during hours and hours of anguished contemplation after she had first hit upon the term "farce". There must have been other times, she decided, when they had been together—at night, perhaps, when she walked into town to meet some students or went to a movie—and maybe when her father went out to buy cigarettes or to visit the tailor, Popperatti. That was what he had told her—well she knew about the cigarettes; the house was always full of cigarettes which her father did not smoke and the visits with Popperatti were too damn long. She knew, and it was all too revolting, but she played her role (as she now thought of it) quite professionally. Like Luisa she danced in the dumb show, hearing nothing, not even seeing all that the deaf woman saw—the plotting.

It was unfortunate that Rosemary had so much time to dwell upon the events of the summer in Italy as they were happening, for her imagery of the stage was confused and tedious, but since no audience existed, she enacted the role of heroine to herself. She was not at all, as she imagined with simple irony, the charming *ingénue* of the *comédie* but the dreary amateur-speaker of long moral poems in the alexandrine turns of high tragedy. She paced the floor, stared out of the dark window, cried in her bed, and nearly beat the heart out of her small left breast—in action more like one of the grand ladies of Corneille or Racine. A scrawny and weak Hermione, she tore at her narrow head in sorrow, passionately conceiving problems of love and duty. Ennobled by her virtue, she vowed that she would go silent to her grave rather than divulge to Anne the sin, her father's final disgrace.

To be practical, Rosemary Sedgely decided it would help to speak to Ennio. Though he was stupid, she thought that the basic drives of honour and love must exist in his sporting vision of the world. It was not possible, however, to talk to Ennio. Occasionally, in the mornings when he drove her to school she would try to scream above the noise of the Lambretta and when he stopped to let her off at the *Università* he had the irritating habit of racing the motor while she said good-bye. Often when he came to dinner he gossiped with Sedgely and Carlotta or he begged Rosemary (and this was the only verbal contact that she could establish) to describe the glories of a Yale-Harvard game. She had gone over it time and time again in minute detail: how the bull dog was paraded about the field with the band playing, and the merry crowd with their whisky and gay plaid rugs, the timeless design of the bowl (like the Colosseum, Ennio suggested brightly). Rosemary would tell him about the Yale-Harvard game gladly because it was the only thing she could think of to say to him—she knew nothing of *calcio* or racing cars and was almost as ignorant on the subject of movie actresses, his third and final interest. So Rosemary confined herself to tales of the big yellow pompoms, the blue and red banners, the price of tickets and, in desperation, feeling very foolish indeed, sang a chorus of Boola-Boola. Each time Ennio was surprised that the ball was kicked so seldom in America. No, there was no talking to Ennio at this point about sin and degradation, but she meant to look up some baseball stories to widen their understanding.

She had, as a matter of fact, just entered the little book shop on the Corso Vanucci to hunt among the American magazines and paper-backs for some information on baseball when she found herself face to face with Abdul Shah Amul. He was dressed in cream flannel shorts and a brilliant red tennis sweater. He stepped back with an almost imperceptible bow and said cheerily, "Hello there! I say you are looking awfully low."

"Yes, I suppose so," she said mysteriously, and then with unfathomable worldly sorrow: "I'm looking for an article on baseball. It's too dreadful, but it's all that hideous Italian boy wants to know."

Abdul followed her to the periodical rack. "How good of you," he said. Through the clipped British accent she felt there was a genuine good will. "I would simply not bother at all."

Rosemary gave him a thin, sorrowful smile, "But I must, you see."

Abdul Shah Amul jogged about, his weak, unmuscular legs dangled out of the creamy shorts like the limbs of a soft doll. He swung two Penguin books about in his hand as though they were a racquet: a recent Wodehouse and an old Angela Thirkell, to amuse himself in this beastly town, he said. Rosemary turned absently through the pages of *Life*, and said how expensive foreign magazines were. Abdul was being so nice to her—it was encouraging and she wanted desperately to apologize to him for her father's

142

behaviour at that embarrassing lunch—perhaps to talk with *him* about the "farce" and how dreary things were.

He twisted his dark head about nervously so that she could not meet his eyes, and finally, looking clear to the other end of the shop, he said, "I say, you are awfully upset about that woman, aren't you?"

"Oh, not really," she gave the sorrowful smile again and put the copy of *Life* back into the *Vogue* pile. "Sometimes things just *are* that way."

"It's nothing you know." He danced up and down as though expecting a tennis serve. "My pater's rather loaded with wives."

Rosemary laughed. How delightful of him to make a joke of it. How kind he was after all and how terribly good-looking. She admitted to herself that the Arabian Nights business was improbable, but perhaps she might have a friend in this Persian, someone to listen, someone to confide in . . . so the sins of her father, Rosemary thought, would not be visited upon her alone. "But now that you are a Christian doesn't it bother you?" she asked earnestly.

"Not actually. One must look at traditions in a larger sense, don't you think? I mean cultures and all that. I may have to give it up back there, Christianity I mean." He pranced to the side of the magazine rack, as though he were anxious to get off. "I've meant to say good-bye. Bad show this town, beastly. I'm to have a private tutor in Rome."

"Oh, how nice! Yes, it is a bad show," Rosemary agreed flatly.

Bowing backwards gracefully and tucking the small British books under his arm, Abdul Shah Amul left the shop. Out on the Corso he breathed a sigh of relief. It had been less tiresome than he had imagined, not difficult in the least. He realized that he owed that poor American girl a dinner or a drive, but really that was impossible. This way, soothing her in a public shop, he had extended himself very nicely thank you. He told himself that he had been *simpatico* : she could want nothing else.

When he had gone, Rosemary stood dazed for a moment, blinded with loneliness—and then she picked up an issue of *The Real Man*. It had a garish cover, a multicoloured scene of scantily clad cowgirls on the plains—revolting—but inside she found exactly what she wanted, an article entitled "The Bush League Breaks". It seemed to be about baseball and there were diagrams and lists of numbers she did not understand.

The next time Ennio came to dinner she was most attentive. First, she went through the routine about the Yale-Harvard game and then performed with her new material. Just as Rosemary had expected, "*il baseball*" enraptured Ennio and she managed to answer all his questions about the distance between bases, the size of the ball, and the number of players with authoritative inaccuracy. After dinner she asked him if he would like to walk out in the garden where it was *più fresca*. He followed her without a word and Sedgely and Carlotta, engrossed in fruit and wine, hardly noticed.

The dead ivy scratched like claws against the tile path as they made their way to a little mound of dirt in the bottom of the garden. There they sat on the dusty ground and through the window they watched Carlotta get up and begin to clear the plates. Moving in and out among the chairs, bending low to reach a dish, her breasts hung round, inviting. Sedgely grabbed at her and she rapped him playfully with a knife.

"*Senta*," Rosemary said to Ennio, feeling that now her task would be much easier, now that they had

144

witnessed this vulgar vignette together. *"Senta,"* she whispered, *"Il mio padre e la sua sorella . . ."* but what could she say about them? He had seen it, damn him, why didn't he speak? Why didn't he rage against them? But no, he sat there expressionless as an ancient statue—athlete at rest.

"Ennio," she began again as though explaining to a child, *"mio padre e sua sorella . . ."* she pointed with a thin, shaky hand towards the house. It was so difficult to say and she could not remember the verb for ruined . . . "your sister is ruined, my father has ruined" . . . *appassare,* no that sounded too much like wilted flowers, *fiori appassati. Finito,* Rosemary decided would have to do. *"La sua sorella è finito,"* she said.

"Come finita?" Ennio turned to her with surprise. His sister finished—what did she mean? Carlotta and Sedgely through? The American professor wasn't going to leave Perugia, leave his sister? It couldn't be!

"Loro sonno amore," Rosemary said. Inside the house her father got up from the table. He and Carlotta moved hand in hand across the room, a light went out, the front door closed and she could hear their voices as they walked out to the road—going to Carlotta's, she thought, filthy, sneaky, rotten. *"Loro sonno amore,"* she hissed at Ennio.

"Si, certo," he replied with a smile of relief. So the professor was not going away, *Grazie a Dio;* he had never had it so good—good clothes, good food, lots of money, since Sedgely had taken up with his sister. So what did this skinny daughter want to say. It was a great puzzle to him.

"Ennio, Ennio," she pleaded, shaking his arm, her thin face turned up to his. He knew—of course he knew about her father and his sister—then why wouldn't he speak, why did he look at her so strangely with those dumb, animal eyes?

"Ah, si. Tu anche," Ennio nodded to Rosemary. This

145

was it; he had worked the puzzle out, though he would never have suspected ... she was so flat and sexless, but the girl wanted what her father had. Ennio caressed her bony shoulder; it might be interesting and a very good deal. After all the professor paid him well for riding her to school each day. He pushed her thin body down onto the mound of earth.

"No, no," Rosemary kicked at him and jumped to her feet. "Rotten, rotten animal," she screamed and then in Italian, "*Cane, porco.*"

"*Cane tu.*" Ennio roared with laughter because that *was* what she looked like, standing above him, panting like a mad dog. So he had guessed wrong. What did she want of him then, this crazy girl? ... him, Ennio, to break up Carlotta and the professor?

Was that that she wanted, stupid, crazy girl? What, did she want him to go back to the old days with cheap food and no wine and Carlotta bitching about every *lira* and the *bravo, Gran Generale* who haunted his life? What did she think, that everything was to be like an American movie, stupid girl? He brushed the dust from his trousers, "*Buona notte, Signorina,*" he said to Rosemary cordially, and went off. She could not see him through her tears, but she could hear his steps, scraping the ivy over the red tiles, and in a few moments the motor of the Lambretta warmed up, gunned, and he was off to town down the Via XX Settembre.

Luisa and Carlotta had both forgotten to light the red vigil in front of the statue of the Sacred Heart. Now the moonlight shone upon Him in a heavenly ray and His white robes glowed with an unearthly luminescence. Rosemary stumbled around the garden path to the niche where He stood, bland and blue-eyed, with every curl in place. "It's not his fault," she sobbed to the statue. It's not his fault." Oh she had been so wrong, thinking of it as a farce, a *comédie*. It was a brutal tragedy to her now (like those plays in English

146

24), in the rawest Elizabethan style, with episodes so distasteful that they should never be allowed upon the stage—the Duchess of Malfi in labour, Lavinia writing with her stumps—it was too deathly, really too disgusting, and her poor, poor father was caught by them, by Ennio and Carlotta and the whole cast, just as she had been trapped at first by their charm and then, only a minute ago by something stronger and more dangerous: Rosemary recognized that what she had felt in that moment when Ennio pressed her to the earth was not fear or hate. It was something else deathly, terrifying: It was desire. "But he is such a stupid, stupid boy." She argued aloud with the Sacred Heart, who gave her no response, and then she struck out in anger at His complacency. The cheap plaster cracked easily; she tore the garment and left a scar directly in the centre of the pretty-boy face.

Albert Sedgely always felt that he must finish what he had begun. In the grey steel cabinets which he had left behind in the library of Lane House, all of his files were, in a sense, completed: the final grades for his students were computed and recorded, the minutes of the discipline committee of which he had been chairman were typed in triplicate, and a carbon copy of each of his manuscripts—the articles on Mrs. Montague and on *Night Thoughts*, and the book on Pope's early prosody were filed away. Though these and other articles could be seen in print, and the book in its binding upon a shelf no more than two feet from the filing cabinet, a copy of the manuscript pages—unsoiled by the hands of editors or Sedgely's marginalia—was filed away in a closed compartment. His correspondence also had its order: there was not a drawer of rumpled letters—no empty envelopes poking out from under a blotter, but more manilla folders—every letter with a carbon of Sedgely's reply, every reply with its acknowledgment. This sense of wanting things to be finished was so strong in Sedgely that it hurt him to leave food on his plate, or coffee in his cup, and he always sat through concerts, plays, and lectures whether it was Monteux conducting the Boston Symphony or Rosemary's kindergarten class in a tableau of the Nativity.

To go through with things to the end was for Sedgely a deep-rooted necessity, so that his coming off to Europe and not returning to the job and wife that belonged to him would seem to leave his entire career, his whole life unfinished. But, he told himself, it was exactly because he felt that life for him was incomplete, and could become something only if he insisted upon it, that he had stayed on for so many months in Perugia. His examination of the metrics of the *Dunciad*, begun over two years ago, he had left in scraps and notes. Paragraphs were half written; pencilled arrows on the typed sheets led to inked observations and corrections at the bottom of the page. Though Albert Sedgely knew that he was an orderly man, a precise man, a fastidious man, the incompleteness of this work did not disturb him. This, too, had been thought out: he should, as a man of feeling, leave things at loose ends if they were no longer of interest to him. But he could not forget—this disturbed him deeply—that at a moment's notice he would be able to pick up the disorderly beginnings of his article and go on. With a single rereading of the poem, he estimated that he could reconstruct his arguments, evaluate the iamb and the wit until the sheets of a new MS were ready for publication. It plagued him to think that his discarded scholarship was still with him, like a line that must continue after its caesura, or the first line of a couplet (which by definition has its rhyme).

Though it troubled him, to know that he could turn

to the past and finish up, he was equally upset about
his affair with Carlotta because there was no end in
sight, no possible finale which he could imagine for
himself and the girl. Sedgely had conceived a passion
for her at first and wanted her, but he did not love
her. It was all without heart: Carlotta was persistent
and fiery as a young mistress should be, and naturally
it flattered Sedgely to have a handsome Italian woman
devoted to him. Her devotion, however, was not all for
Albert Sedgely as a man—he was a *professore*, an
Americano, qualities which to Carlotta were as virtu-
ous as truth or bravery, qualities which were as attractive as ungreyed hair and a young body. She loved her
Alberto so well that when he kissed her on the forehead or patted her on the shoulder with that distant
look in his blue eyes she knew that he would rather
have a cool glass of mineral water than make love to
her or that he was tired and would leave her soon with
another fatherly kiss. It did not disgust Carlotta that
Alberto could leave off his role as lover and become a
weary man with a white moustache, a man like her
own father. As a matter of fact it was to his advantage for Carlotta's father had been a *gran generale*,
a man *molto bravo*.

Her knowledge of history was sketchy and highly
personal so that when she spoke of old Manzini's hero-
ism in the invasion of Albania, she spoke proudly and
without irony. He had been a major then and had
led his troops, well-armed and well-trained, against
the surprised Albanian peasants, defending themselves with farm implements and old boards. She remembered well how her father had come home from
Albania for a week—just like a business man who has
been to Milano, or Turino, he had come home from
war, a huge soldier with silver-white hair and a white
moustache, dressed in a perfectly tailored uniform. At
dinner his face had flushed red with anger because as

149

he went through Bologna on the train he had seen banners of victory and heard the music of parades. When he changed trains in Florence people were dancing in the streets and the students were drunk and singing, while, Manzini said, the soldiers of Italy were still dying at the front. Personally, he found the wine in Albania so poisonous that he believed his liver and kidneys were rotted out. Carlotta remembered that she could not play while her father was home from war because he slept during the day. At meals he drank enormous bottles of Aqua Fiuggi and two full litres of Umbrian wine, to clean out his system before returning to the horrors of the battlefield.

In the North African campaign old Manzini had proved his worth as a soldier once again, and just two days before he surrendered his men to the British, a confirmation of his appointment to the rank of general signed by the hand of *Il Duce* himself reached him in the desert. In prison he had been treated with the respect due a high-ranking officer—that is what he said when he came home to Perugia after the war— but his liver and his kidneys were again rotted, this time from the English food. He was still a big and impressive man who wore handsome suits—they were always military in cut, and a blue triangle sprinkled with general's stars was always stuck into the lapel.

Carlotta told Sedgely that her father was this *bravo generale*, but that he was not a Fascist. "No," she said credulously, "my father said that he never agreed with Mussolini, not even in the beginning." That is what Manzini would say at times, but more often he would look startled when he heard the great leader's name and try to recall out of the annals of history, the unfamiliar Mussolini or the *Fascisti*—as though from centuries ago. He thought he remembered, but not in detail—the way one might recall that Boadicea had once been Queen of the Britons. Old Manzini died

(Carlotta could still cry and describe the coffin with the flag of Italy draped over it and the coloured rosettes) after a few years in retirement—from lack of attention and disappointment; none of his internal organs were impaired.

To Carlotta, her father having been a hero, none of the young men in Perugia seemed quite good enough—or perhaps old enough, or honoured enough —so that Albert Sedgely had become her friend and later her lover; he was a distinguished and older American gentleman. In this way she did not compromise her ideals: she had worshipped her father to such an extent that any man of value would have to remind her of old Manzini whom she had nursed until death. She never mentioned this to her Alberto, because her father had looked so worn and sad towards the end, and besides Alberto was not nearly so tall, and he was not a military man.

To Sedgely, who knew well enough that personal relationships cannot ever, unlike letters or scholarly articles, be completed, his affair with Carlotta seemed unnecessarily static: his loveless attraction to her dragged from one dry, hot day to the next. It could never end, Sedgely knew, even if he were to pack up and take himself to the Yucatan, or off to the Foreign Legion on the most fanciful escapade, because having known anyone as closely as he had known Carlotta— or Anne for that matter—it does not end, but shifts, turns about, and goes on. He wished that it could all be like a film strip, hundreds of blocks of almost sameness, but run through a machine, speeding by, taking him off the scene mechanically, painlessly. Before Rosemary had come to stay with him in Italy, he had not felt the strain of making love to his Italian mistress; now he knew what he dared not guess many months before—that no true emotion would *ever* come of his already dying, now tediously repeated, passion. It had

151

seemed correct during the lonely winter and lush Italian spring to delight in the fullness of Carlotta's body and her dark plentiful hair without caring for her in a romantic sense. It seemed part of the way he should be in that larger life which he was enacting. Now, in the long summer drought he began to sicken with the incompleteness of his feelings for the girl; he was unable to love.

At night he would tell Rosemary that he was off for a stroll to buy cigarettes or he would wait until she had gone into town to meet some of the students, and then he would walk down the road slowly, swaying from side to side as though he had grown fat in the past months; then he would stop momentarily, and contemplate the dust on his pointed shoes or absently twirl the tips of his white moustache. Soon he would sway on again, making his way cautiously along the road like a heavy old man who stops for breath and strength. But Albert Sedgely was in his early fifties, trim and in good health: he stopped on the way to Carlotta's to put off for another instant the disaster of his own insufficiency.

The Manzini house was much larger than Sedgely's but in advanced decay inside and out. When the *Generale* lived, it had been nearly a *propria villa*, but for years there had been no money to keep it up. Beyond a rusted gate the yard was cluttered with dismembered machines and dusty tires which Ennio had played with and discarded. The laundry was everpresent: a line of enveloping nightgowns and the bright sporting shirts of the Perugia soccer team stretched from the front windows. These clothes, dried stiff by the sun and with no breeze to move them, seemed to Sedgely stylized, as if cut out of cardboard and pasted up for scenery. Tiles had slipped from the roof and lay rusty in colour as the parts of old motors on the heat-cracked earth. As Sedgely waited on the dirty stone steps, he could always hear Carlotta's high heels resounding on the marble pavement of the halls as she came to open the door, apologetically, for a great carved door should be opened by a servant. The first time he called upon her she lied and said that the *donna di servizio* had gone home to the country for the day; but actually there was never anyone to open the door but Carlotta because Ennio was far too lazy. Later she had had to tell Sedgely the truth; crying and smothering her shame in her long black hair, she told him that there was no maid to go to the country, had not been for many years, and that she washed the floors and the clothes with her own swollen red hands. It was a disgrace for the daughter of General Manzini: she would not wash the front steps or clean the rubbish out of the front yard though, because the neighbours watched her.

Before Rosemary arrived on the scene, Sedgely seldom went to the Manzini house to be with Carlotta. Now, of course, if they were to be alone at all he had to visit there. It was a tiresome routine which made his evenings seem as uninspired as his mornings—waiting for the tub and pots and pans to fill up with water. When he came on a summer night to Carlotta's house they would stand for a moment inside the great door while she admired him and welcomed him in the effusive manner which she associated with a fine lady. The Manzini house was filled with big rooms that seemed empty. Each room was like the next, high ceilings, age-streaked walls, huge unsilvered mirrors hung in tarnished frames. Heavy pieces of furniture carved of dark wood sat about in formal poses, but did not begin to fill the rooms. The bareness of the walls was broken only by tinted photographs of Carlotta's father in his many uniforms or by reproductions of the Virgin. There were no draperies on any of the high, dusty windows. Sedgely wondered at first if there had

153

been large pictures or more furniture or perhaps carpets that had been sold, but since there were no bleached squares on the walls to show where paintings had once hung and the parquet floors were all equally worn, he presumed that this was how the house was intended. In the best days the Manzini could hardly claim nobility, nor were they truly wealthy, so that these barren, weightily furnished rooms represented their short-lived elegance. On Sedgely's first visits to Carlotta they had sat facing each other on faded satin chairs in one of these big reception rooms, but now they passed through the echoing marble hallway to the back of the house where Carlotta had her own bedroom, and where she lived.

The reality of Carlotta's poverty was more apparent in her room than in the rest of the house: it was a cheerless place crowded with sentimental scraps of her life. A feminine smell of cheap cosmetics lingered about the daisy-papered walls and the veneered bedroom suite. The mirrors were bright and cut around the edges with futuristic designs of the nineteen-thirties. There were innumerable snapshots pinned up—mostly of old Manzini posing with two or more of his officers in their fancy uniforms. A few photos pictured him next to a thin, pale creature with the face of a peasant madonna, and in these Manzini was a young man wearing the shabby suit of a clerk. Sedgely supposed that the pale woman was Carlotta's mother who was never mentioned: he heard only of the great man who had not befriended *Il Duce*. There were snapshots, too, of Ennio receiving prizes—victorious, holding a crash helmet or a soccer ball under his arm as though it were a second head—he smiled at the camera with the vacant look of an exhausted athlete. More recently Carlotta had added pictures (which she took with childish pride) of Sedgely—Sedgely sunning himself with Popperatti in the café, Sedgely merrily

154

raising a wine fiasco *a la campagna,* or (the one he now could hardly resist tearing to bits) Sedgely slightly drunk, unwisely prompted to imitate one of the carved griffins in the main square. It was all of her life thumb-tacked to the wall; her father, her brother, her lover —these three whom she had been trained to champion with the pride of a parvenu and worship with the submission of a medieval peasant.

On the biggest mirror over her dresser, Carlotta had stuck a rosette snatched in a moment of passion from her father's open grave. The red of Italy had faded to pink and the green was paled to yellow. It reminded Sedgely of a disagreeable custom which Rosemary had at boarding school; pinning her corsage ribbons, trophies of some prep school dance, to a bulletin board. Once Carlotta's girlish mementos had been charm-ing, but since Rosemary's arrival he could not stop drawing the obvious parallels between his daughter and his mistress. Many of the irritating adolescent traits in Rosemary's behaviour now became apparent in Carlotta.

There was, for instance, the new lamp in this room. Sedgely had convinced Carlotta that he preferred to talk in the dark so that when he came into her bedroom he took great delight in turning off the bare light bulb which dangled from the ceiling—not that a lover's words are more naturally whispered in the dark, but the night hid the cluttering scraps of memory, the photos, the daisies, the religious cards that danced be-fore his eyes in disturbing patterns. But now, with the new lamp in the room, they argued. Carlotta had gone to Upim, with Sedgely's money of course, and bought a *tipo moderno* lamp with a green ameobic-shaped base and a pink ruffled shade—a lamp which she adored—a lamp which left no corner in the shadows but bathed the entire room in rosy splendour. Sedgely turned it off; she cried. Sedgely turned it on again; she pouted. And the lamp nagged at him as though Carlotta were saying what she was far too good and simple to say : "Once I could do anything I wished, before your daughter came. Now I can do nothing right, now that she is here and you have become ashamed of me." She demanded constant attention, sincerity and love from him—very like Rosemary, even more adolescent.

One evening that Sedgely was to remember as hotter than any other during that summer, they all four had dinner together—the Manzinis and the Sedgelys. After the meal Rosemary and Ennio went out to the garden. This pleased Sedgely because he knew how trying Ennio could be, how idiotic and limited he might seem to his daughter. He was also pleased because Rosemary had made an effort which he interpreted as surprisingly humane : during the meal she talked constantly with Ennio, amusing him with stories about football and baseball, and though she had her facts confused (five yards for a first down, fifty feet between bases), she was so spirited, trying to establish a rapport upon what for her were shaky grounds indeed, never once did he detect a patronizing tone. Yes, Rosemary was more cheerful that evening at dinner than she had been in days, in weeks— since she had brought that despicable Arab home, Sedgely thought, since she had unfortunately discovered that Carlotta was his mistress. He had found her behaviour in the interim most objectionable. She played at being a heroine, tight lipped and long suffering; but that night, he thought, her spirits were seemingly revived.

When they finished eating, the two young people had wandered out while he and Carlotta lingered over the last of their fruit and wine. Then she began to clear the table, moving in and out among the chairs and once, Sedgely remembered, Carlotta bent low stretching for a plate, exposing her breasts—exquisite objects. He grabbed at her and laughing, she rapped him on the knuckles with the flat of a knife blade.

Not long after his daughter and Ennio went into the garden, Sedgely and Carlotta left the Villa Carina and walked down the road together hand in hand. They turned into the Manzini yard. "Damn it!" Sedgely cursed as he tripped over a large metal object.

"*Ah caro, caro,*" Carlotta whined. It was Ennio's fender—the fender of a Fiat *Mille Cento* which he had brought home today.

"Stupid kid and his junk," he said in English.

Then, as though she understood, Carlotta said in a soft, cajoling voice, "*Ma lui è un bambino ancora.*"

But Sedgely would not be appeased. "*Ennio ha venti anni,*" he snapped and limped up the front steps. He thought that he would never reach Carlotta's little bedroom in the back of the house. She turned on the new lamp and helped Sedgely to sit down on the bed. Carefully she rolled up his trouser leg and folded down his sock. Across his left ankle there was a long red gash and the surrounding flesh was already turning blue and puffy, but although the skin had been badly scraped, nearly exposing the shinbone, Sedgely did not bleed.

"*Ooo, che peccato,*" Carlotta moaned and then made him stretch out on the bed. She was soothing and experienced: she fluffed the pillows and dashed in and out of the room with wet towels and ice cubes from the small refrigerator which Sedgely had bought for her at Christmas; and as she tended his wound she began to sing a little song—a religious song from her convent school days. Sedgely understood that it was about the immaculate heart of Mary. It was quite clear to him as he looked about in the glowing pink lamplight and saw the snapshots of General Manzini on the wall that Carlotta was happy in her role of nurse, and that he lay on her bed to command the beautiful child-woman who sang to him and bathed his painful ankle. She broke her song to moan with infinite sympathy, *"Il poveretto . . . Alberto mio."* Now as she bent over his raw flesh he could see in her eyes how she loved his wound and he could see once again her heavy, warm breasts which (before the incident of the Fiat fender) had stirred his stale desire. Sedgely twisted his head on the pillow so that he would not have to watch her. She was fussing too much over him: it was nothing more than a bad scrape. The next time she left the room he sat up and rolled down his trouser leg. He would tell her not to fuss, not to make a project out of his little mishap; and later Sedgely recalled that he had meant to say to Carlotta when she came to minister again, making him feel old and ill and impotent, that she made him nervous flitting in and out with ice and wet towels.

But, then, when she did come back and looked at him full of remorse, he did not have the heart to speak sharply to her. Instead he said something which he had not planned to say at all: *"Carlotta,"* he had said, *"Io sono un povero."* And surprising himself, though he had never told Carlotta what he lived on, he had explained to her that there was no more money; and this was true—it was nearly all gone, their savings, his and Anne's. There would be barely enough to pay Rosemary's college tuition in the fall. He supposed that this had been brewing for months, brewing secretly like some irresistible poison to be drunk when in despair—and that he, having spent like a Renaissance prince, without further lands or jewels to sell, should now be able to drink his princely cup with honour.

And Carlotta cried, kneeling at his feet, raising her hands in supplication—her fingers cracked and scarred with scrubbing, thickly crusted with the yellow calluses of her laborious years. *"Lavorerò, lavorerò,"* she cried, and Sedgely could see that she was overcome with joy . . . I will work, I will work for you, and her face was radiant with tears. He would come and live with her and she would care for him. She would cook and wash and find a job at the sweater factory or the candy factory or in a shop. Sedgely saw himself washed in the deep-pink sentiment of her lamp, pinned to the wall along with the fake hero-father and the profligate brother, and he saw himself again, looking out from the mirrors, put down her hands and kiss her paternally upon the forehead where that richness of black hair curved down simply and perfectly into a widow's peak. And he could see himself still, photographed as a fool—aping a mythical beast tacked within her daisy-papered prison, and, turning, he was visible again, reflected life-size as he got up from the bed and walked away from her unquestionable beauty and from all the submission and sacrifice which he knew would make Carlotta's life complete.

"I must go. Tomorrow is one of those early mornings to run the water." Albert Sedgely practically ran out of her little bedroom, *all without heart, all without heart* resounding through the hallway, out through the great front door. He leaped over Ennio's fender and was half way up the road to his house before he remembered that he had spoken to her in English. "Well," he thought, "it can hardly matter. That is the slightest fraction of what she will not understand."

Suddenly his ankle became extremely painful. He stopped for a moment to look at it and then hobbled the rest of the distance to the Villa Carina. His small Italian house was in darkness as he entered, and it was an afterthought that made him go into the kitchen rather than directly to his bed. He thought that if he took those large pots and the big kettle into the bath-room and left them there overnight, then in the morn-

159

ing he would not have to traipse through the room where Rosemary slept and she would not hear him crashing about. It was such an efficient idea that he wondered why he had never thought of it before and why he thought of it now—the picture of Carlotta in mind, kneeling, weeping, praying to consume him. He hopped on his right leg through the darkened living room and found the light switch just inside the kitchen door.

Rosemary's body was stretched out on the floor— and his first impression was her shape, how thin she was, the spindly legs and arms a distortion of the human form; and for all her length when he picked her up she was light as a porcelain figure. He turned her body over and her unconscious face was peacefully dumb as the thin-headed dog she had always resembled. Her breathing was light and relaxed so that only the big carving knife which lay beside her and a cut in her blouse gave evidence of anything more violent than a gentle sleep. Albert Sedgely saw that his daughter had managed to raise the knife and make a stab—a very weak attempt it must have been—at her shallow breast. There was no blood, not even a scratch in her flesh: the knife had been stopped short by her padded rubber bra. Now he rubbed her wrists vigorously and slapped her cheeks, a method of revival which he had seen in movies, and suddenly the scene had a quality about it that was rehearsed, and Sedgely knew that he would never be able to distinguish between the amount of play-acting and the amount of reality which had gone into this moment. She came to life with an ungainly jolt and began to cry, turning her face down into her father's embrace Rosemary sobbed and sobbed, "I tried. I wanted to. I tried."

"Yes, yes," Sedgely rocked her in his arms. "Poor little girl. Poor little girl."

"And then . . . and then I think I fainted."

"Yes, yes." He thought (for he had read it more than once) that there was an enormous difference between the motivation for the successful and the unsuccessful suicide—and that this child whose golden hair he caressed was truly miserable with the first knowledge of her premeditated failure.

"I tried. I tried," Rosemary wept.

"Yes, yes. We tried. We tried." He lifted her bloated, tear-stained face and said, "Poor little girl, my poor little girl."

VI

ELAINE GREEN WAS FURIOUS BECAUSE FIRST OF ALL she had gone over there just to be nice, and besides she *had* to get out of the house. Phil was correcting galley proofs all over the living room floor and she and baby Sally could not even *walk* through their own house, not to mention talk. And this, of course, was all because the library was like an oven in August, and so she didn't blame Phil for taking up the entire living room, which was the coolest place in their small apartment, but she just *had* to get out so she got all ready in her yellow cotton dress and put Sally in a fresh sunsuit and decided to go over to Carol Perkins'. She was absolutely furious because of what Carol had said and because she had gone over there to be nice.

It was a nice day, too, in spite of the heat, and Phil had been very sweet when they left. She and little Sally had gone tippy-toe into the living room so as not to disturb him and she had said in just the *tiniest* whisper, "Give Daddy a big kith bye-bye." Phil had been really darling and given them each a big love, one for his baby girl and one for his baby wife, and he had taken the torn galley sheet out of Sally's little fingers in the most understanding way. Poor little thing didn't know it was special and important and besides those long sheets were the strangest looking things—she couldn't imagine how they ever got a normal book together after printing it in those strips, and she said that to Phil and he said, "article not book."

Well she and Sally had gone over to the Perkins' at a snail's pace, as Sally had just begun to walk and

Elaine wanted her to do it all by herself without the stroller. And she had gone to visit Carol because Carol was her friend or at least she *thought* so, and because she hadn't seen Carol in about a week and Elaine had gone over there to be nice. First of all, Carol came to the door and looked surprised as though she couldn't imagine what Elaine and Sally could possibly be doing on the front porch—as though it were the White House.

"Oh, Lord," Carol Perkins said in a very funny way. "I wasn't expecting you." As though *she* had called up every time she came over for coffee with little Sam. Finally she asked them to come in, and right away Elaine noticed how different the living room was. All the toys were gone, all the fuzzy dogs and plastic rattles and the cute bells—even the bird mobile was down from the ceiling. Instead there was a typewriter on the coffee table and lots of books and papers and the biggest dictionary she had ever seen outside of a library.

"Well, I haven't seen you in thso long," Elaine said, "and I shouldn't have come out becauthe Phil is up to here," she indicated her smooth ivory neck, "with those old galley proofth."

"They finally came. Oh, Sam will be delighted to hear about it," Carol's rodent face lit up with enthusiasm. "Don't you think all the tortuous hours of rewriting seem worthwhile when the galleys arrive?"

Elaine replied brightly, "My, yeth," and settled herself on the couch and wouldn't let Sally get on her lap because of her nice crisp yellow dress. And it was then that she really had a moment to notice how funny Carol looked—like she used to look, in a drab old seersucker dress and her hair all screwed back into a little knot, except that it wasn't long enough and the ends flew out in the messiest way. Also the grey showed terribly in front where she had not touched it up or been back to the beauty shop or done anything at all to it. Which, unconsciously, made Elaine find a blue plastic comb in her purse and run it through her own shiny hair which was yellow, almost matching her dress and that was why yellow was almost her favourite colour unless it was light blue which matched her eyes. But Carol Perkins looked terrible, so she asked, "How have you been? I mean, I thought you might be sthick or sthomething sinth you didn't call."

And Carol Perkins with mouse-like intensity said no, that she was in excellent health and scurried about collecting the papers—which turned out to be her manuscript—and even took the sheet out of the typewriter and then put them up out of reach on the mantel, which Elaine thought quite unnecessary: Sally knew never to touch paper with writing on it—if it was a normal size. "Well, where ith my little darling?" Elaine Green twisted her pretty head about coyly, "Where's my little Sammy?"

Then Carol had said the first funny thing: that Samuel, Jr. was now on a new schedule; "a convenient schedule for all of us," that is what Elaine remembered her saying. The poor little boy was supposed to sleep all morning practically so that Carol could be free to work or type or whatever she was doing. Elaine asked: "Well, what if the baby ith crying?" and Carol said: "Too much attention can be destructive," or something like that and that he, meaning the poor teeny baby, had to learn to live in "an ordered universe."

"My, yeth," Elaine agreed perfectly, and because she and Carol had been such good friends, or at least she had *thought* they were, she had asked—just to be nice, "Carol, didn't you go to the beauty parlour again?"

"No," Carol had said decisively. "I shall not go again."

"Well, you know, you could uthe a rinth at home. Everybody does, except maybe Mrs. Sedgely who doesn't have to. I mean thse doesn't have to think about four or five dollarths." And Elaine had suggested *that* just to be pleasant again, so she was really surprised when Carol, who looked absolutely grey-faced without any lipstick on, said:

"No, I must suffer with my hair. This unnatural dye will grow out."

"Oh, Carol. Oh don't be thilly." Elaine wailed, and it was then that Carol Perkins said the really funny things to her.

"No, Sam and I have discussed the whole problem at length. I must continue my work in philosophy. It is best for him and best for me in the final analysis, and though it may not seem so at the moment, we are sure that it will be best for the child." As Carol stood in the centre of the room, explaining things slowly to Elaine, gnawing at the words, bobbing her compact head in and out, she seemed with her stripes of grey hair growing through the black dye like a busy chipmunk, and even Elaine thought that she was like some small animal. And calling that sweet little boy "the child" wasn't *human*—very remote and cold and not what you would expect of Carol.

"You see," Carol Perkins said, "I have my work which cannot be discarded as though it were a frivolous pastime. It is not as though I had been hammering silver jewellery all these years, or weaving placemats."

"Well thertainly not!" Elaine pursed her baby pink lips sympathetically. "Why Mrs. Johnson didn't even *have* the thilver clath last year."

Carol darted across the room and rescued the Oxford English Dictionary from little Sally, or Sally from the Oxford English Dictionary which, of course, made little Sally cry until Elaine found a piece of Holland Rusk in her purse and then Carol had said the next funny thing, and Elaine had thought that she said it in a very prissy kind of way, "Try and understand, my dear." She bit at the words with protruding incisors. "I have my work, and my work is what *I* have to give to my child."

"Yeth," Elaine said, but she didn't understand at all because there were several faculty wives who did work in the library or the administration offices to earn a little extra money but she couldn't figure out how just typing out these things on philosophy on the coffee table would be very profitable.

Then Carol Perkins softened her manner and spoke slowly, as though she were reasoning with a naughty child. "But you do understand, don't you, that if one is to work one must go on a schedule? What I mean to say is that any Saturday afternoon after two o'clock I would be most delighted to see you and little Sally."

"Well, my, yeth," Elaine smiled her prettiest young-mother smile. "Dear it must be late. Thilly me, I could just talk forever and poor Phil thwamped with all those nasty proofths." So then she picked up little Sally and she said, "Bye-bye, say bye-bye," at the door and Carol Perkins was already getting her papers and the O.E.D. down from the mantel, before Elaine and her little girl were even all the way outside.

Samuel Perkins, Jr. shrieked in protest while his mother put the half written sheet back into the typewriter; but her thoughts were muddled now and there was some kind of beast in the machine which made her fingers strike the wrong letters. She sat back, a sad and wistful mouse, to reassure herself: if she went upstairs and took the baby out of his crib there would be an instant of fulfilment—an instant which she had vowed to resist, because it would lead to the hours and hours of frustrating nothingness in which she had no identity whatever. The baby's shrieks died into spasmodic gasps—he was learning, he was adjusting, and soon he would be quietly staring at his feet or sucking on his tight little fist. She was sorry that she had put things to Elaine in such a straightforward manner and she remembered how elated she had been when she and the baby first went to visit her and chat and play with little Sally. Most of all Carol Perkins found it strange that she, who concerned herself with the basic problems of freedom and desire, should be finding it difficult to accept the verifiable. She and Sam had discussed it at length: her mind had been numbed by the emotional excitement of childbearing and mother-love and then the unsuspected period of boredom, the long days of diaper-washing and baby-joggling that she had not been able to sustain. Though her fingers trembled as they hit the keys, she typed on.

In the afternoon Elaine Green just had to get out, because Phil would not pick the galley sheets up from the living-room rug, which was the only cool place for Sally to play, so when she and little Sally went out visiting she told her friend how funny Carol had been that morning. Carol Perkins, she had *thought* was a "real human being", so it was very hard to understand how she could say all those things—"not real human being"—and she had never even offered her a cup of coffee, and Elaine who was furious now, had gone over there in the first place just to be nice.

Part of the legend that surrounds Will Aldrich is that he never takes a vacation. This is not strictly true, but it seems so because the duties of a college Dean do not end when the spring term ends, and it seems true because it is easy to believe any legend about a man who is white-haired and handsome and intense— a man everyone in the community knows more as a public figure than a private personality. So it streaks through the offices of College Hall like summer lightning when Will Aldrich announces to his secretary that he wants to get things in order so that he can leave for a week at the end of August to see his sister. Within a few hours everyone in town hears that Will is taking a vacation and this in itself is such news that no one notices that Anne Sedgely is to visit friends on the Cape during the same week. There is no scandal; no one ever knows.

So Anne tells Mrs. McCabe to stop the milk, pull the shades, and oh, yes, if it doesn't rain to water the nasturtiums which are blooming gaily along the front path. And that night they (Anne Sedgely and Will Aldrich) steal off to New York together—such lovers as the town will never see. On the way they stop for gin-and-tonics and finally arrive at their hotel at a suspicious hour in the morning. The desk clerk yawns at them and the elevator boy—having just delivered a fat salesman, a bottle of Seagram's, and a red-headed Negro woman to the eighth floor—hardly notices the discreet middle-aged couple he picks up next. Then Will and Anne read the numbers on doors as they walk along the carpeted corridor and find their room, 689, and enter their own neatly-prepared nest.

Anne, taking the wrapper off a miniature cake of soap says: "I feel so perfectly anonymous. This is a wonderful idea."

They discover that they have *coloured* television in their room and that the glasses are sterilized and wrapped in cellophane and so is the toilet seat. With ice water and bourbon from a flask they toast in air-conditioned bliss to all sorts of splendid days and happy nights. Anne Sedgely wears her white nylon slip as elegantly as a Chanel tea gown. She lifts her sleek brown head to be kissed and says that they must drink to the glories of room 689, which is the only place *she* ever wants to live again. They do not fall asleep until four o'clock, and when they get up it is nearly noon. They find a copy of the *Herald Tribune* outside their door and order big glasses of orange juice and bacon and eggs to eat while they get dressed.

Some days they go to galleries and museums, or Saks and Bonwit's. Other days they take a bus down Fifth Avenue and walk around the village where Anne buys a Japanese tea pot and Swedish candlesticks which she says will look horrendous in Lane House. Once they lunch at Chambord and afterwards Will insists that they go to Tiffany's, where he buys Anne a circle of gold leaves with pearls for buds and pins it on her black linen suit. Sometimes Anne looks up, at dinner or in the middle of a play to assure herself that Will is still across the table or beside her, and naturally enough he has not disappeared but smiles at her or takes her hand. And Anne thinks that he is the most beautiful creature that she has ever seen and knows that people turn to look at his face and remarkable white hair. One day in the lobby of the Statler they turn a corner together and in a mirrored wall seem to walk towards themselves. "Two beautiful people," Anne says, meaning it for a joke, but knowing that it could be said without irony.

At night they lie in one another's arms and tell how their lives happened. Will Aldrich was brought up on a farm in the Mid-west, which Anne remembers hearing many times, but it does not seem real until this moment. "It's so strange," Anne says. "You have to make moos and chicken noises to convince me, because it so far from anything that you are now."

"That's not true. My farm life makes me a successful dean—I was good with animals, so I am good with boys." And then he says how hard it is to grow away from the past, and yet for so many people how unlikely the past becomes.

"Not me," Anne says bitterly, knowing how closely she has kept the traditions of her family.

Will loves her and wants to comfort her. "You had a better beginning." But later that night, Anne Sedgely

169

dreams of Lane House—dreams of not being able to climb the graceful staircase—a dream somehow involving the George II teapot melting over the Hepplewhite sideboard, and the house itself which *is* Lane House and *feels* like Lane House stretched into narrow passageways so that Anne cannot tell what room she is in. And in the morning she tells Will: "Isn't it disappointing to be a simple creature. We talk about the past and immediately I dream of my house distorted."

And still another night Anne loosens the knot of Will's tie with her long, manicured fingers and asks him when he started to love her.

"The possibility was always there, but it was at the Scholarship Bazaar."

"Good Lord!"

"Well it was spring and you were pathetically nervous about the whole affair—whether it would go, with all the Elizabethan trappings; but you were conscious, too, of the foolishness involved, and more upset really about Rosemary going off to Italy than about Greensleeves or the mulled punch."

"I don't sound attractive," Anne says.

"There is nothing more attractive to me than a charming lady with big problems." Will Aldrich manages to sound like a clergyman making jokes about God, and Anne Sedgely begins to understand why he is the white-haired biblical leader to all the lonely and sad boys from Shaker Heights and Scarsdale and the lonelier, sadder boys from Malden and the Bronx—because he is able to love them and to care about them. And this capacity to love seems so enveloping to her that she feels at times that she is not with any ordinary being or in a real world, though naturally enough she is pleased with herself, that she is able to return his love with an alarming passion. Anne thinks of all the ugly little boys with overbearing mothers and all the scared handsome boys with pregnant sweethearts and knows how easy it is for them to come into Will's office because you can say anything to him.

At last, with hesitation, Anne says: "I don't have enough money to pay Rosemary's tuition for next year. I thought I might get a job or sell some things quietly to an antique dealer."

"Don't worry about it," and his hand touches hers in a sympathetic gesture. "I'll take care of it."

"No," she says to him quickly, "I can't take money from you."

"Don't worry about it."

But Anne has the final word; she whispers, "I can't."

Their week runs out, and when they leave the city she finds the key to room 689 in Will's pocket and they have a lovers' quarrel because Anne told him that she put the key in his pocket and Will can't remember because, Anne says, he was not listening. She is sorry and says that they should be like Pierrot and Pierette and have a wonderful time making up. Then she sings to Will—scraps of popular songs that she remembers, *Dancing in the Dark, Deep Purple*, "Button up your overcoat," Anne sings, "Take good care of yourself, you belong to me," and suddenly it occurs to her as a whole new problem ... belong, belong. What a queer, upsetting word and she decides that she is querulous and edgy because their heavenly vacation is all over—but as they drive north, farther towards Massachusetts the night air begins to smell like September air for the first time and Anne says it is a new beginning. It is nearly two in the morning when they arrive home and the entire town is dark and unseeing. Lane House, as they turn into Anne Sedgely's street, is blacked-out, self-contained, and makes her feel for a moment uninvited.

"Oh, damn Mrs. McCabe," Anne says as they walk up to the front door.

Will laughs at her, "But you haven't set foot inside."

"It's my nasturtiums," and she pulls a long, sorrowful face to see the limp plants along the front walk. Standing in the hallway she brightens up, remembering her dream, "Well the rooms aren't squeezed out of shape anyway."

"What?"

"Nothing," Anne says, because it doesn't seem important enough to talk about.

In the living room Will picks up the accumulation of mail and says, "Here's one from Rosemary."

"Oh, fine." Anne reaches out for the letter—"but let's have a drink first—a nice long bourbon and soda."

And when Will returns from the kitchen with their drinks she stares at him like a woman crazed, her eyes unblinking, wild.

"They are coming home. That's what it says, that she is coming home with Albert." And she finds that she cannot lift her numb hand to take the glass which Will holds out to her. "It is all wrong."

"No." He is priestly towering above her, "It will work out just as well this way. Wait and see, Anne, it will work."

"But Rosemary is bringing Albert home," Anne repeats.

"That is what you sent her for."

"But how was I to know ... it's too horrible, it's all wrong."

"You must tell him at once, Anne, and then we will leave."

"I couldn't." Anne Sedgely shivers and withdraws from the touch of her lover. She feels beaten, dazed, and yet she knows that Will is trying to tell her that he would throw his whole life up for her and that she must go with him, leave everything that has ever existed for her and go with him. She feels Lane House under her feet and sees that Mrs. McCabe has swept out the fireplace at last—very softly, so that it is barely audible she tells him, "I can't do it."

"But you have proved that you can. It wasn't just a matter of needing someone, or being lonely, or being bored. I am sure of that."

Once again Anne says, slowly, carefully as though he has not understood: "They are coming back."

"What did you think would happen?" Will asks.

"I didn't think," Anne cries. She tries to look at him and lie. "But I think now that it was unreal, our life in 689." His white god-like hair looks fiery and his eyes are furious with love, and she wants him more than ever.

Will Aldrich thinks, "You are lying to me. It was the only real life you will ever have."

And Anne, as though she has not heard him, says, "It will become unreal as time goes on, it will grow farther and farther away from anything I know and it will seem like a neurotic middle-aged dream or like a play we have been acting—like one of those clever plays with only two people."

"We have not acted together—" he finds it difficult to say, ". . . That's a rare thing, not to act with another person . . ."

"A pretty speech," she says.

But Will goes on: "All the rest of our lives we go from pose to pose, not hearing, not listening—our voices are drowned out."

"What do you want of me?" Anne grows shrill, holding herself stiff and defiant. "What do you want? My husband and my daughter are coming home. You expect me to walk out the front door with you into the supernatural moonlight, back to the eternal bliss of a hotel room."

"You're twisting it. It makes it easier."

And Anne Sedgely, almost screaming, doesn't hear. "Well I can't. I'm not like you. I'm not a saint," and

173

her voice breaks so that her final words to him are low and throaty, "I'm not a goddamn martyr. I can't."

Will Aldrich smiles with true and yet ironic benevolence, "Ah, then there is nothing more to say," and he turns from her and leaves the house. Anne listens to the door close, the car start, and knowing that it is too late she runs out of Lane House (now warm with the glow of electric lights), out into the front yard as though she might still catch him, and crying aloud she throws herself, she, Anne Sedgely—Anne Lane, that is—onto the dead nasturtiums now cold and slimy with the morning dew.

And the next day his secretary looks at Will Aldrich and the news goes through College Hall with meteoric speed that he has been on a real tear, and by afternoon people in town are taking sides. Some say that they don't believe it and others say that a man, even Will, has to let go once in a while so that he can live.

Abdul Shah Amul and Ennio lay in the sun at San Remo. The sand was a glittering white and the ocean a travel-poster blue. Abdul Shah stretched his brown limbs unconsciously, pleased as a lazy cat, and opened his eyes ever so slightly so that they were slits through which he saw that Ennio, Allah be praised, was still asleep. This whole affair was a wow, a fantastic success and Abdul enjoyed every moment of his triumph, except for those unfortunate times when he was left alone with the handsome Italian boy—who did not, as the Americans say, speak his language.

It had been pure genius, actually, for Abdul Shah Amul to have thought of Ennio Manzini and he was delighted with himself. He had left Perugia in the beginning of August and gone to Rome, only to find that there was no one there at all ... and an American who had been at Balliol with him, a chap by the name of Gold (of course, that had been rather embarrassing

174

because he had thought the chap's name was Silver)—
in any case he had run into this American in Rome
who had said as much one day: that there was no
one in the city worth speaking to. The story had its
own amusing twist, because naturally Abdul Shah
Amul had never spoken to Gold at Oxford, but "when
in Rome" and all that sort of thing . . . he felt that he
might as well let the barriers down because the chap
was quite right—the city was empty, positively void.

And now, as Shah Amul flicked a gnat off his red
bikini, he could not help smiling to himself with
pleasure, because when he had first arrived at San
Remo he had been so hopelessly naive, so "out of it", as
Gold said. It reminded him of those unhappy days
when he first arrived in England to be educated, a
pious Moslem boy with a trunk full of ready-made
suits from Regent Street: he had had an incredible
amount to learn. Yes, his debut at San Remo had been
as unpropitious as his arrival in England, but now
here they were, he and Ennio, the biggest *thing* of the
season—indeed, Abdul thought, glancing down in
admiration at his own mahogany body, they *were* the
season at San Remo.

And he told himself that one learns a great deal at
Oxford but then of course when one goes out into the
world, as it were, things are rather different, aren't
they? He learned that when one is to *live* in a place
it isn't as though one were simply to go about looking
at paintings and monuments and churches, is it?—
and he was to live in Italy, forced to actually, because
his father insisted that he get that wretched degree in
architecture. He still could not understand why his
father did not hire someone to build the filthy hotel
for him, but his father had the childish notion (all un-
educated persons do) that one was made useful by an
education—as if he had been sent off to learn a trade.
Forced, Abdul Shah Amul had selected Italy as the

country in which to study architecture. He wrote home to his father in Persia that there were many famous buildings, and he comforted himself with the knowledge that the scholastic requirements were much less tedious in Rome.

Given this fact, that he was to be trapped in Italy, the whole affair was quite amusing and a really good show. He and this chap Gold were sitting on the Via Veneto one evening and Gold said that he was going down to San Remo to see his mother and that it might be a frightful bore but nothing could be worse than Rome in the summertime—unless it was Paris. Abdul Shah Amul had agreed with a sigh and so Gold said that he might come along. They drove towards the Ligurian Sea the very next day—Gold in his Jag and Abdul in his Alfa Romeo.

It was embarrassing at first for Shah Amul, rather awkward as a matter of fact, because there were a good many Marchesas, Counts, Infantas and such at San Remo so that being a Shah seemed hardly to matter. No one cared about his father's oil lines or the proposed hotel—no one listened when he said he was to study in Rome next year . . . at the *Università* . . . *architettura.* No one even noticed his Balliol blazer so expensively tailored on Savile Row. He was terribly on the fringe and could only stand by and watch: there was an extraordinary amount of drinking and undressing. Actually, it was a Mexican film starlet just zipping out of her ballgown, who said the first kind word to him, "I hear you're a Sheikh, lovey."

She had a peculiar accent, Abdul thought, almost cockney, and then, so as not to show his amazement at the areas of white flesh which she had uncovered, he said with an air of weariness, "That is correct, my dear, I am indeed a Sheikh."

"Well, that's awfully too bad," the Mexican film starlet said.

176

"How's that?" Abdul Shah Amul asked.

"Your being a Sheikh, lovey, because that was *last* year. I mean we were *filthy* with Arabs."

"Really!"

"Oh, my, ain't it turned out warm." She began to unhitch her underwear, "Whew, too damn hot for my money."

And then there had been the mortifying business of Mme de Haigh-Gomez, ex-Gold, introducing him as a Rhodes Scholar from Topeka. It was so desperately embarrassing at first that Shah Amul was prepared to return to Rome and study Italian, and he would have done just that if he hadn't had his magnificent idea, a stroke of genius, really, about the *Cento Milia*.

Every conversation that he overheard seemed to be about the *Cento Milia*. People were mad for it, and just to prove Shah Amul's own point about how "out of it", and how badly innocent one could be, he actually had to ask Gold, *sotto voce*, what the *Cento Milia* was. It turned out to be a frightfully dangerous auto race which went on at Brescia and everyone was entered—or placing bets—and there were to be some marvellous parties. Gold said that his mother, Mme de Haigh-Gomez, felt that the season went limp at the end of August—whether she was at Cannes, or Viar-réggio, or Capri, it didn't matter—everything fell to pieces on her—so this year she had thought up the *Cento Milia*, that is, she had made it into a *thing*, so that it would be a grande finale, an absolute *festa*. Gold confessed that his mother could not take complete credit because last year the race had become quite popular, *post mortem*—several of their dearest friends met tragic, untimely deaths.

Abdul Shah Amul said that it was an amusing idea and that they could certainly count him in. Secretly, he was terrified. He did not drive very well and he envisioned himself turning up as an obituary notice on the back of the page with the Mayfair dinner parties, or, worse, his father might get wind of the escapade and order him home. Well, there he was in an absolute fit of depression when he had had his inspiration. He remembered Ennio—that dull, athletic type in Perugia, the one involved with the vulgar Americans. As it turned out he could not have had a more fortunate idea: Ennio was wild to drive in the *Cento Milia* and when they returned to San Remo together they were a sensation—an absolute *chose*, which merely pointed out yet another time how much one does have to learn. Abdul Shah Amul was the only young man at San Remo that season who had a really pretty Italian boy.

To say that his having Ennio was a success, a *coup*, was an understatement: they were wined, dined, pursued through the streets, and he was booked-up well into the New Year. Mme de Haigh-Gomez was enchanted with young Manzini—she could not keep her hands off him. "This kid has a beautiful body," she said clutching what she so admired.

"*Lei è molto gentile, Signora,*" Ennio replied, detecting a compliment in her voice and manner.

"He's like a statue, like some gorgeous statue of a god or an animal." And then tossing her head, such a metallic blonde head, like an old-fashioned coquette she explained to Ennio, "*Lei è un dio giovane e animale.*"

It was all quite gay now at the seashore, Abdul thought. He let the glittery white sand run through his toes and reminded himself that one can not be too cautious. He decided, for instance, that it would be dangerous to visit in Paris with Mme de Haigh-Gomez, ex-Gold—ah, she was delightfully amusing while one was on holiday but she was the only woman he had ever met who managed to wear real jewels so that they simulated paste—and then too, she was just beginning a new, soul-wearying business about mahjong. As for Gold, he wasn't a bad sort really, but Shah Amul was pleased that his own Oxford career was over—it would never have done to know him there. He sat up now and looked out at the sea. It was the bluest water he had ever seen, a blue that might be accepted as Nature, but would never stand up as Art. Yes, the Riviera sun was a delicious drug, but he could not lie here forever. Smiling, satisfied with himself, he drew a deep breath of blue sea air and thought that one should never keep a beautiful lady waiting, should one?

He turned his heavy-lidded eyes to see if Ennio— *oremus*—was still asleep, for avoiding young Manzini was the only difficulty in this whole successful affair. The boy seemed to think that he, Abdul Shah Amul, must have a genuine interest in auto racing and talked endlessly about *"la macchina"*, and Stirling Moss and Fangio. There were moments when Abdul Shah Amul almost wished that he *did* have a desire for Ennio, that the boy might be more to him than an employee—it would have made the whole situation more bearable. Unfortunately, he felt nothing but a growing distaste for Manzini, and he finally told him. in broken Italian phrases, to buy all the tires and crews and helmets that were necessary for the race, but not to be tedious about it. Now Shah Amul blinked through the bright Italian sunlight, squinting, uncertain—ah, splendid. Ennio, who had been up half the night "doing things" to the motor of the Alfa Romeo, slept peacefully on.

Abdul Shah Amul slipped into his kimono and stole off to meet the Mexican starlet for a private cocktail.

The *Cento Milia* was a really good show. Aside from the messy business of Ennio driving into a ravine ten miles outside of Brescia, there was never a dull moment. Shah Amul did the handsome thing and went to the hospital next day. He regretted that Mme de Haigh-Gomez insisted on going with him and creating a scene.

"This kid had a gorgeous body," she cried, pressing her metallic curls into Ennio's unconscious face. "This kid had the body of a young god."

Abdul Shah Amul thought that it was disgraceful, the manner in which the little sisters of Salvator Mundi had to wrench her out of the bed and the shrieking as she was dragged from the room. "I want him ... I want that kid to come to Paris with me." And she screamed so that the little sisters would understand, "*a Parigi, a Parigi il dio giovane.*"

Shah Amul was outraged—such bad form and she was still wearing her soiled *décoltage* from the previous night's festivities. It made his own visit to Ennio less affecting, less *simpatico* than he had intended. He questioned the doctor in a voice that was solemn and subdued and was truly relieved to hear that Ennio would live. There seemed to be some complication about damage to the spine, so Abdul Shah Amul made out a splendid check—to be drawn on the Bank of England—and arranged personally for him to be transported, eventually, to Perugia.

Still, he was depressed as he left the hospital with Gold's mother—her large emeralds looked obscene in the daylight, flashing like pieces of green glass on her crêpey throat—he could not bear to look : her make-up formed orange rings around her scaly eyes. It was bad luck really about Manzini and now his lovely holiday was coming to an end. Soon he would have to settle down in Rome and learn all sorts of tedious things about structural concrete—what an awfully bad show. He was sick at heart about the Alfa Romeo —such a jolly red car—he had grown quite fond of it, actually.

VII

WHEN THEY BROUGHT ENNIO HOME IN THE AMBULANCE
Carlotta held him in the pose of a *pietà*. She went
mad; and lifting his body off the stretcher as though
he were a child, she held his strong athlete's torso to
her bosom and let his legs, his poor dead legs, trail on
the ground. Crying until Ennio's face was wet with
tears, she thanked God, the Virgin, Jesus, the Holy
Mother Mary, and all her Saints who had brought
him back alive. They (the ambulance attendants from
Brescia) carried him then into her own daisy-papered
room, the finest room in the house she said, and nearest
to the refrigerator.

Carlotta nursed her little brother. She washed him
with Castile soap and fed him the best *filetto* in
Perugia. She brought him cool drinks from the refrigerator and she sang to him: comic songs about soldiers and wine and fat mammas, sad songs about
lovers who were leaving in the night, holy songs about
angels and about Mary conceived without sin. And
sometimes, when Ennio was not himself, he said cruel
things to her—then softly, gently, she whispered
"*Zita*", or "*Ringrazia, ringrazia Dio.*" Secretly she
thanked God when Ennio talked the dirty-mouth, because then he reminded her so much of their father,
the *Gran Generale*, whom she had nursed in the same
bed and who said those dirty things too. All day she
stayed by Ennio's bedside, and at night she dozed fit-
fully upon a rusty iron cot outside his door, getting
up a dozen times to gaze into the darkness and listen to
his even breathing, coming and going—his peaceful

sleep. Early, while his beautiful dark eyes were still closed, she would steal out to the first Mass at San Giuliana and pray to God and light a candle to the Virgin.

And when she was at Mass—*Maria, Madre mia,* how she wept for his poor dead legs, and knew that it was a curse upon them for their sins—but Ennio was still a baby, so it was a curse upon them for *her* sins, because she had loved Alberto who was already married and not a Catholic. She was being punished for her sins, and for Alberto who had never loved her statue of the Sacred Heart. She had placed the statue in his garden so that Jesus would bless the house and bless their love, but she and Alberto never went into the garden during the long, dry summer. It was as if she had asked Jesus to stand there in the hot sun and bless the weeds and the dusty trees. Carlotta dropped *lire* that she could not spare into the poor box to make up for it—to herself she confessed that she loved Alberto out of pride, because she was the daughter of Manzini, the great general, a man *molto bravo*, and her lover was *il professore*, an *Americano*. It was a great sin and she was being punished for it, and Ennio, *il poveretto*, was being punished with those poor dead legs—she thought that it was a curse upon them and beat at her breast, *mea culpa, mea culpa, mea maxima culpa.*

Carlotta Manzini is one of the women of this earth who become more beautiful in sorrow. It is only in pictures of Magdalene redeemed that the tear is an iridescent jewel upon the cheek and the cheek itself is not withered, the mouth not distorted with anguish —and Carlotta too was lovelier than ever as she knelt in the simple church of San Giuliana. The first lights of dawn shone upon her through the rose-window. Her luxurious black hair was drawn back from her face and she wore a tattered veil of black lace that

182

had been new for her father's funeral. The prayers of a beautiful supplicant, of a Magdalene, are usually answered in one form or another, and so Carlotta's prayers were heard, or, to put it more accurately she knew that they were answered and she prayed in thanksgiving—mingling, as a child does, spirituality and practicality—and that in turn becomes another prayer of supplication: the process is recurrent.

Early one morning it began to rain in Perugia. It was the middle of September and the drought ended. By the time Carlotta reached San Giuliana her clothes were soaked and the pale dust had washed off the olive trees that grew along the road. She thanked God because she would have all the water that she needed to wash the sheets, to cook for Ennio and to bathe him. At Mass that morning she knew that her prayers were answered: God had given Ennio back to her, with his legs that would not move; and it was a blessing, because he could not go off again and be brought back to her dead—yes, and it was a blessing that Alberto was taken away before Ennio was struck down. How could she have worked to earn money for Alberto and nursed Ennio at the same time—it was wonderful how God gave his blessings, and she thanked Him.

In the light of these blessings she saw for the first time how things could be. The doctor said that Ennio would not walk again so, newly inspired, she prayed to the Holy Mother that she might have a wheel chair for her little brother. She could lift him into the chair and then she would wheel him into town. She could wheel him to the café and he would visit with his friends—then, he would not be so lonely and he would not say those bad, dirty-mouth things. There was so much to hope for she told the Virgin: she and Ennio would both grow in grace and be worthy children of General Manzini. Towards the end of Mass, when she stood for the Last Gospel, she had figured it out in detail—Ennio would have a little shop, with an espresso machine, a licence to sell *tabacchi* and perhaps, God willing, a lottery for the *Totocalcio*, a sport which he had played so well. He would be able to wheel himself around the little shop and she would take him in the morning and go to get him at night—it was a great and God-given blessing.

And then she prayed after Mass, when she lit her daily candle to the Holy Virgin Mary, that she would be pure again and good and that she would find money for the wheel-chair and the Immaculate Mother would send her money for the shop and the *tabacchi* licence —and she knew that she had sinned in loving Alberto out of pride; it was a great sin but she told the Virgin that Alberto had loved her and had loved Ennio as though he were a son. *O Maria*, her heart was spilling over with joy, because God works in strange and mysterious ways and she knew then that Alberto was a blessing, too. She would write to Alberto who had loved her and he would lend them a little money, just a few American dollars.

The red vigil light flickered before the statue of the Holy Mother, and Carlotta cried and thanked God, for now she could see how her prayers would be answered and she thought how beautiful it would be if she could also have a *televisione*, for Ennio, her poor brother who could not walk. She would put the *televisione*, a small one only, on her dresser; she would light her new pink lamp that made the room warm and pretty, and then Ennio could watch the sport events which made him so happy in the past—she would write to Alberto. On this first day of rain God had heard her prayers and He would bless Alberto, and Alberto would not forget his children.

As she left the church that morning, Luigi Rocetti came towards her through the rain. He was on his way to work in the Porta Marzia, but now the season was over for him. With this cold, wet weather the tourists always stopped coming—at least they didn't come to him to see the famous underground street of the great Baglioni family—they went to the dry picture gallery, or the Etruscan Museum. Rocetti turned up the collar of his ancient checkered suit and thought how rotten it was that the rain had come this early —some years when he was lucky it didn't rain until the end of September or even October. As he came up to the church of San Giuliana he saw Carlotta Manzini, and he stopped, pressing the marcel in his greasy black hair. "*Buon giorno, Signorina.*" He smiled at her with his rotten, nut-coloured teeth and reached out towards her as though to touch her hand.

Carlotta did not answer. It seemed to her that he had been waiting for her, waiting outside the church, hidden and evil . . .

"She is now more beautiful than she was before," Rocetti thought, "before that buffoon of an American had her." And he wondered, letting his lustful eyes wander over the fullness of her body, whether now that the American was gone, now that she was left and her brother was a cripple . . . He put his damp, nicotine-stained fingers on her hand, "*Allora,*" he said in the low, compelling voice that he used to draw tourists into the Via Baglioni, "*allora, il professore è partito . . .*"

But to Carlotta he was an apparition of the devil, a filthy little animal of the Baglioni caves, and her soul still filled with the actual grace that God had sent her, she spit on the ground. Who was he to touch her, the daughter of General Manzini, the sister of Ennio who had been struck down with God's blessing? Then she called Rocetti a devil and told him to go back to his cave, to go under the ground. Who was he to speak to Carlotta Manzini. Yes, Alberto had spoken to Rocetti and even taken coffee with him, but how

185

was her Alberto to know, *il poveretto* who had loved her and been like a father to Ennio? She thanked God as she walked home in the rain, God who had saved her from the devil, and she prayed again and knew what she must do.

She would go to the Villa Carina and take the statue of the Sacred Heart, and she would pack it carefully in straw and send it as quickly as possible to Alberto in America so that Jesus would bless him and watch over him. She would write to Alberto about the wheel-chair and the *televisione* and she would pray for his eternal soul.

The Sedgelys were having a late breakfast when Mrs. McCabe came into the kitchen. "The man is here with the flowers," she said.

Albert put down his coffee cup. "What flowers?" he asked.

"Chrysanthemums for the front steps," Anne said.

"Well, where do you want them?" Mrs. McCabe's voice was petulant.

"Oh, tell him to leave them around front—around by the front door. I'll plant them this morning." It is really quite unbelievable, Anne Sedgely thought, that after all these years Mrs. McCabe can't figure these things out for herself, and she knew from the look on Mrs. McCabe's face as she left the room just how rudely she would tell the man from the nursery to put the flowers around front.

Albert went to the stove and poured himself a second cup of coffee. He looked a thin, professorial gentleman with white temples and pale eyes. The only thing remarkable about his clean-shaven face was its colour, a deep bronze tan that made him look as if he had just returned from a vacation. "Isn't that bad for you to do all that gardening?" he said to his wife. "Won't it bring on your allergy?"

"No, dear, only roses in the spring." She thought it peculiar that Albert should have forgotten that it was only roses that brought on her rose-fever, but she had to be careful with him. He seemed to be his old self, but then every once and a while something like this came up, some detail he had completely forgotten. "If Rosemary doesn't get up soon I shall have to call her. Today is her last day, and as far as I can see she hasn't begun to pack her trunk."

"Well, she was out late." Albert smiled sympathetically. "I meant to ask you last night—who was that young man who came to get her?"

"Braddy Wilcox." There, he's done it again, Anne thought.

"You mean *that* was Bradford Wilcox—that young man with the limp?"

"Yes, he had an auto accident last year," she told him. "It was a hideous business, too much beer and a sports car of some kind." The telephone rang. Mrs. McCabe came into the kitchen again and looked directly at Anne, "It's for you," she said.

Albert Sedgely ate the last bite of scrambled eggs on his plate. They tasted odd and he imagined it was because they were the first scrambled eggs he had eaten in over two years—but not many things *were* odd to him or strange. It was all coming back too quickly, and soon he would feel as though he had never been away—like he felt when he had first seen Anne again : she was exactly the same, the same handsome face and neat brown hair, even the black linen suit he remembered. Tomorrow Rosemary went off to college, and in a few days his own classes would begin. He tried to look forward : in his course in the Augustan Poets he usually gave an introductory lecture, an intellectual background of the age, in which he talked about Locke, the classical influence, the Great Chain of Being ... It was not his kind of lecture—

great sweeping statements—thumb-nail sketches, but he had always felt that you had to ease them into it on the first day. Strange, he could not remember the order of the lecture—it began with a quote from the *Essay on Man*—

> Born but to die, and reasoning but to err;
> Alike in ignorance, his reason such,
> Whether he thinks too little or too much;
> Chaos of thought and passion, all confused;

but how does it end and then where ... ah, never mind it would all come back. And thinking about his course reminded Sedgely of his discarded article on *The Dunciad*, the metrics of *The Dunciad*, and he felt that he should take it up again and finish it—because it was the only thing that he could properly do ... and he thought, finally, about the arthritic body of Alexander Pope, the twisted little satirist with his enormous capacity to hate—but to hate with beauty, with passion—and Albert Sedgely envied him.

When Anne came back from the telephone she looked distressed, so he asked, "Who was that?"

"Honestly," she said, "I don't know why I let myself in for these things. It was about the Christmas Bazaar —they want me to be chairman."

"Well if you don't want to ..."

"Oh, I don't know," she hesitated. "I just don't know what I want to do about it. Basically I hate bazaars, but I said I would think it over." Then Anne felt that she had to explain, because Albert had not been here last spring, so she said, "You see they want me to do the Christmas thing because last year I ran the Scholarship Bazaar and it went very well. I put a lot of time and effort into it and it was a great success."

"Yes, Rosemary mentioned it."

"It was all done Elizabethan," Anne said. She began

to pick up the breakfast dishes and pile them in the sink. Then she remembered the chrysanthemums and thought that she had better get to planting them. When she ordered them from the nursery she told the man that she wanted nice tall ones, an even number of yellow and that lovely russet colour—it was just the colour of old brick. In previous years she had ordered the russet colour with white—which matched the red brick and white trim of Lane House—but she had decided that the yellow would be much gayer, much more exciting, and she believed so firmly in changing these little patterns. She turned to Albert, still sipping his coffee. "I must get those plants in this morning."

"Well," Sedgely said, stroking his top lip, as though there might be a moustache there, "I must get to work, too."

Anne went to the cellar to get her gardening tools and her quilted knee pad, and when she came upstairs and walked through the front hall of Lane House, the ancestor portraits, all the fusty old people, she thought, looked particularly approving that morning. All those grey-faced old people, descendants of Mathias and Sarah Lane like her, seemed to have unattractive smirks lingering about their straight, hard mouths. Wouldn't it be wonderful to take all those boring old faces down and put up some bright, forceful abstractions—large canvases that were all colour and line and involuting shapes. But the Lanes had been there so long she imagined that they would probably grow back, like huge nightmare fungi, right through the contemporary paintings until their stiff, fusty faces reappeared on the same dark backgrounds. She stood for a minute at the bottom of the stairs, her hand caressing the newel post as though it were some tactile sculpture, and thought that she should call Rosemary if that trunk was ever to be ready to go off to college tomorrow. "Rosemary, Rosemary."

"She's in the bathroom," Mrs. McCabe yelled. "I heard the tub running."

"Oh," Anne said to herself and went out the front door. It was a sunny September day and the town was coming to life: to her left some students were playing on the tennis courts for the first time this autumn, to her right the stack lights were lit in the cinder block addition to the library, and from the rear —no more than twenty feet behind Lane House—she could hear the first boyish obscenities of the school year from the Delta Phi lawn. It was all going to begin again, she could see that, and there was no way for her to stop it. She decided then, irrevocably, that she would run the Christmas Bazaar—after all, why not? It would fill in so many blank hours—why not? It would give her a means of organizing the days: it would be like the spasmodic running about of chickens who do not know that they are dead. Yes, she would run the Christmas Bazaar and do it all medieval.

Anne Sedgely looked down, and there in the bright autumnal sunlight were her chrysanthemums. The yellow ones were just as gay as she expected and the russet ones were precisely the colour of the bricks in Lane House. But she found that they were no comfort to her at all.

So when Rosemary came downstairs for breakfast, almost at noon, she found no one around, neither Anne nor her father, and she was just as glad because she couldn't bear to talk to anyone—not after last night. It was too divine, last night; she had her first date with Braddy Wilcox since her return from Italy and it was all so marvellously different—not the way she had remembered it, deathly dull, but absolutely perfect.

There was no coffee left, so she went to the icebox

and poured herself a glass of milk. God she was really glad Anne wasn't here to start the business about packing her trunk. She could be alone and remember how it was last night, and she did remember the exact way she felt when Braddy had come into the living room, limping, and she had looked for an awful moment at his leg, and then she had looked right into his eyes.

There was a moist, white line on her upper lip from the milk she was drinking; it made her mouth childlike. She drifted about the kitchen, opening cabinets and drawers, and at last found the bread box where it had always been ever since she could remember; but she was not conscious this morning of such dreary things—not after last night—and sighing, Rosemary dropped a piece of whole wheat bread in to the toaster. She thought of how it had been later when they had gone to a little place to have a beer and there was some deathly music playing and she realized that she and Braddy Wilcox would never dance together again —it was so incredibly sad and really symbolic what had happened to him. Now he was wonderful and it seemed to Rosemary that it absolutely *had* to happen, what had happened to both of them.

Then Braddy told her how it was all the long, bedridden summer when his leg didn't heal right and had to be all re-set and put in traction for all those horrible weeks, so he had started to read a lot of French poetry which he had actually sort of liked before, but now he read it again—Mallarmé and Verlaine and *Les Fleurs du mal*, and he was perfectly divine when he told her about it. She decided that she would take a course this term in *Le Symbolisme*. And then later they were in the car and Rosemary described the whole summer in Italy to him, the University and the Villa Carina, and Perugia, and she told him all about her father and the revolting business with Carlotta and Ennio—all the things she could never tell Anne, or anyone else. Her narrow face glowed with joy and she thought that it was too much to ask, really, too wonderful to be true, that her father was back in Lane House, that her father and mother were together again.

Mrs. McCabe came into the kitchen to start the lunch and Rosemary asked, "Where are my mother and father?"

"He's in his study. Your mother's out in front with those flowers." She looked at Rosemary and said disagreeably, "Are you going to eat that toast or let it go to waste?"

And Rosemary thought that actually Mrs. McCabe was about the most limited individual she had ever met in her life, but it just couldn't matter this morning because everything was so marvellous after last night —and it was exactly the way she wanted it in Lane House, quiet and so divinely normal.